CONFESSIONS
OF A BYEONTAE

CONFESSIONS OF A BYEONTAE

BYEON BYEON 변변

byeonbyeon

Copyright © 2026 by Byeon Byeon Imprint
Book layout by JBookDesigns

For information, please contact Byeon Byeon Imprint at
byeonbyeon@confessbyeon.com

Printed in the United States of America
ISBN: 979-8-9922135-6-0
First Edition: 02/26

CONTENTS

CHAPTER ONE

BORN AGAIN

AGE IS BUT A NUMBER

One of the first things a Korean will ask you is myeoch sal-ieyo (몇 살이에요), which means 'How old are you'?

To a foreigner, it doesn't seem friendly. To a woman, that's double down. But there is a reason for that. Their culture dictates respect by age. Unless you are born in the same year, which makes you friends, everyone else is older or younger, senior or junior, family or not. Making it hard, I imagine, to meet a love interest or form a relationship across ages.

Being of Chinese descent, I still maintain some aspects of Chinese culture. The Chinese language has levels of respect, although not as complex as those in our East Asian counterparts, such as Korean. As English is my first language and I've lived in the US for most of my life, I'm a Twinkie. Sometimes, I feel that way because I am an immigrant in the land of the free, more Asian than American-born, bringing the culture and the languages of my childhood. And yet, when I'm in Asia, I am the foreigner, a lone cowgirl in the grasslands.

So, how old am I? Smart enough not to tell you. South Korea, though, my label would be Ajumma (아줌마), and there was no way to escape that horrendous title.

Ajumma

A derogatory term reserved for married and over-middle-aged women. Some portrayed with tightly permed hair, visors, and mismatched clothing to hide from the sun, her pack of cackling friends, and their fierce opinions.

Descriptions of these women vary depending on where they lived, but one thing is obvious: Korean women do not want to be called that, and neither do I.

And he said it, "Ajumma." Pointing with that judging finger in ridicule. Across the Pacific, in a bedroom somewhere in Seoul, this young man laughed. To him, I had the nerve to be there, watching him. I was some spoiled fruit, pathetic, and a fool.

Never have I ever felt this slow burn.

He skipped me, and that was good riddance. Frozen in a spot, I stared at my laptop. Closing it and burying my head in my covers as my heart bled. My ego, which once was whole, was stabbed with a shade of black.

I had no feelings for that stranger. I didn't know his name or where the fuck he was. But a bruised self wasn't quickly healed, and for the rest of the day and a half, I mulled in seething anger at that one word and the derision on his handsome face.

Was it wrong for me to be there? It was my first foray into on-line chat after years bundled in a bubble of suburban life. So what if I was chatting with people younger than I was? Was it wrong to want to feel the rush of freedom and be who I am?

They didn't know me.

Age is but a number. This soul could fly free. And in my first bout of freedom, I was shot down for being too old.

The Koreans were an enigma. Though we were Asians, their Confucian thinking and group mentality differed from mine. Where I was and where I am now, our societies were cosmopolitan. In America, with various foods, skin tones, and religions, it was difficult to comprehend the monoculture.

My curiosity grew with K-pop and K-drama blaring through

the Internet and on our TVs and music apps. Were they how the media portrayed them? I knew I shouldn't trust the media. Like Hollywood, the Korean machine was well-oiled and excellent at producing the dream-like entertainment everyone was addicted to today.

I wanted to know. There had to be more to them. Underneath the kbeauty, perfect bodies, and hot moves, these people were normal and had the same urges as I did.

I wouldn't let one jerk stand in the way of my exploration. My excitement burst through. Ometv, the random search chat app, was my gateway. YouTubers showed me how I could get the Korean experience they had. The truth was at my fingertips. I wanted to know.

This Ajumma was going to prove a point. I wasn't going to let that cruel word get me down.

"Who said I was a has-been? Milf is the hottest searched word, and this Ajumma is only just beginning."

WELCOME TO MY HAREM

"Congratulations, Second Husband!"

It started as a joke because of this Korean guy. He called many times a day after our first online sex act. Always horny and wanting more. I showed him my pics and vids — my ass being pounded doggy style by H, my boobs grabbed with H's choking hand, my moaning as my climax rose, and many dirty acts.

"Have you heard of ahegao (アヘ顔)?" he asked one day.

"Ahe what? What's that?" I asked.

"A Japanese word. Face during sex." So, I googled it. The faces were weird. Cross-eyed with tongues sticking out. It won't be surprising in manga and anime, but seeing it in real life was a little disturbing.

"Okay…why?" I asked, even though I already knew what he wanted.

"I like that. I like seeing a woman's face at climax," he said.

"I can't show my face," I told him.

"Why?" he asked.

"Same reason why you don't show your face." I tapped on my shades. The Internet was a vast ocean of darkness, and I was a clueless bird flapping too close to the waves.

As a prank, I told him that I was masturbating in the library behind the shelves. That got him excited. He was persistent, and at some point, he trusted me enough to show me his face, so I showed mine. He loved it so much that he said, "Wow. I want to get married."

"With who?" I teased.

"With you. Haha," he said.

"With me? I'm already married. Unless you want to do a three-some with my husband and me?" I joked.

"Haha. If it were close, I would have gone right away, whether it was a threesome or with you."

"Really?" The tease backfired.

Today was Christmas, and Santa brought an unexpected gift.

"He proposed to me!" I whispered excitedly showing H my phone.

"Can we do it now? Vid chat?" Second husband was asking. The texts flashed, rolling up as he kept going, and then my phone began to ring. I shut it off immediately.

This was weeks after we decided to be Open. After coming out to my husband, H, about my online affair and agreeing, we would work on trying out this new life of dating and sleeping with others.

Was this Korean guy serious? Far across the Pacific, a young, handsome, single man in his twenties wanted me to be his wife.

Was he expecting me to visit him in Korea and consummate this relationship? Instantly, I was reminded of the Asian royalty and their concubines. Except, I wasn't a King or noble. Yet, the thought of a second husband in Korea was mind-boggling and thrilling.

He was the first to take a dick pic for me when I asked for it, and despite his protest, he gave me my first cum shot too. It was a trophy that I treasured and played with.

He could be the start of my harem. It was that spark that ignited a crazy idea. At that time, I had two IG accounts for my Korean friends from OmeTV, separating the guys based on danger zones. They came and went — my young fish were looking for fun, someone to chat briefly with, and others were just lonely.

Life was the same every day. House. Kids. Errands. Cooking. Mom friends. Nothing was ever new or changing — a forever state of stasis. But after I met those stranger twenty-something-year-old Korean guys and entered their rooms every day, adrenaline rushed through my veins.

"When was your first sex?" I asked the first guy I met for the day. Asking to play was becoming a routine. Meeting a stranger, staring eye to eye as I took off my clothes, was as natural as taking a shower.

The mornings after dropping the kids off at their schools, I would dress in my lingerie, preparing for another round of flash and play. Hands jerking. Cum exploding. Korean faces I met whom I didn't know, and many I may or may not see again. But the first faceless one, I still remember.

I won't forget his words, "My teacher was very hot."

It was amazing that with translators, I could easily talk to a stranger about his sex life. We shared our secrets and said whatever we wanted without fear.

"There is no judging. I don't judge," said another guy.

Back to my vivid imagination of my first. A student in the chemistry lab where the two illegals performed the deed. Even today, a teacher like her could be judged as abusing her authority, but she was a dream come true to many boys and men. He sat on a chair by the window, and she climbed on his lap.

"Omg. Did it hurt?" I was told it might. Boys have skin, but with circumcision, maybe it was easier the first time."

"No," he said. "It was so good. She was so wet."

"Daebak! Damn…your teacher!"

His smiley smiled. "We did it many times. I cummed in her."

I imagined I was there in that science lab. Long tables with high stools. Sinks at the far end of the table. Beakers in wood stands. A table in the front where his teacher sat.

The naughty teacher with that tight skirt and no panties broke all the rules and did what her profession made her swear not to do. She was in the back seat by the window with her student, ionically bonded as two atoms became one.

Now, that was some special treatment. After school, extra tuition. Every pervert's dream.

This guy won. Clearly, he did — reality vs. fiction.

"How long did you meet her?" This was a full-blown illegal activity and not a one-time act.

"A few months…and then I graduated," he said.

"Ahh…why did she choose you? Are you handsome?" I asked because I wouldn't know; all I saw was his stiff rod. That and him asking for my boobs and breathlessly cumming.

Months later, I think I met him again. Randomly, I decided to check the vid app again to get some ideas for my story, when a guy said, "Byeontae Ajuuma!" and smiled. "How are you?"

He was a handsome guy with boyish looks. He could easily be part of one of those K-pop groups and have a massive million-dollar following. I remembered thinking, what was a guy like him doing in an app like this?

"I'm good," I replied, still trying to place him and slightly annoyed by the Ajumma label.

"Still playing games?" He smiled and spoke in good English.

I nodded and narrowed my eyes.

"You're wearing sunglasses now," he said.

"Yeah. Do I know you?"

He grinned. Too cute. Messy combed-down hair with shiny moonlit eyes and smooth skin.

"Yes…you know me. But I'm not playing today."

"Oh, that's fine." I'm still trying to make him out. A guy like him should stand out. It was impossible that I didn't remember him.

"Have fun! Go find some game." He waved and clicked off.

Now, thinking back, I bet it was him — my fifteen-year-old virgin-who-lost-it-to-his-teacher. Only he would call me Byeontae Ajumma. I changed the game to Byeontae game after the first play because I felt that I shouldn't label myself.

The Ajumma label would likely get lost in translation with the Koreans, who would not understand the subtlety of my sarcasm or the struggle to break free from labels of age and stereotypes.

Many months have passed, and it was getting closer to the day I was heading to Korea, my big pilgrimage in June.

Seoul — my dream, my bucket list to jump on as many Korean guys as I could. The land of my fantasy.

"Second husband." I grinned as I typed excitedly when he logged on again.

"Don't call me that," he told me when we started our vid chat.

"Second husband? Why not?" I smiled. "But, it's the truth. You're my second husband. You proposed to me, and I said, 'yes'." I teased. I always like to tease him like that.

"Stop calling me that," he said, cleaning up his white sticky mess. We had fun again after a long time, and it was good.

"But why? It's sweet. Our in-joke." I sensed a conflict coming. Like all marriages, the honeymoon was ending. "You're not my real husband if that's what you're worried about."

"I know, but I don't like it. Don't say it," he pouted. "Why are you chatting with other men? You are going to have sex with more than me in Seoul?"

"I'm Open," I said. "It's my bucket list. You know that," I told him.

"You should only be with me."

"I'm sorry. I didn't have an Open relationship with H to be closed in Korea," I said.

My heart shrank. He wasn't in lust with me anymore. We weren't having fun and talking about whatever we wanted. No filters. Anything that came out of our mouths. After the first time we met, it became clear he lusted for more. The phone was endlessly ringing, and he demanded the next high.

He wasn't the only guy I was reeling in. Each wanted my time. For each one, I orgasmed, and we enjoyed ourselves. They went to sleep relaxed, and I started mine happily, sixteen hours behind them.

But harems didn't last forever. The followers swish like the waves that ebbed. Fishes came, and fishes went.

Lust hurts. Lust scars.

I had my share of ghosting. Over those months, their hurt took time to recover because, despite how I tried, my soft heart wasn't made of steel.

Our cultures were different. Those promises and words of love and affection were lies. Like a naive little girl, I wanted to believe them because I always told the truth. Much as I played, I didn't promise something I couldn't keep. In the end, I realized it was all part of the game.

If I wanted to play this, I had to be stronger. It was challenging trying to understand the minds of these men, who were both foreign and exciting.

The Asian mind.

I was more American than I thought. There was a cultural divide. Being Open was hard for Second Husband to relate to. The freedom to do what we wanted because our independence and differences mattered more.

Each time my Korean friends left, my heart steeled. Metal bars prevent the leak of compassion and sadness.

"You're more mean now," I was told.

"I'm just joking," I replied. "Getting them to laugh gives me a high."

"I know. But you're more mean now."

Something had to give. I was trading my pure soul for this. The sweet innocence and the comfort of being in a cocoon of family life from these dangerous waters. I was getting hurt and, each time, scoring a mark on my unblemished skin.

As the months went on, it became a little less painful. I wasn't going to stop. With pain came pleasure, and the benefits were high, and the fumes of ecstasy were hard to stop.

Forget Second Husband. Forget the promises he made and never kept. Forget he'd come back, but he didn't. I, on the other hand, would always be here. Behind the dark screen and in that chat app I'd always been on.

One day, if he returned, even if he ghosted, I would welcome him with open arms. Not because I'm cheap and needed him, but because I am curious. What lives did they lead after they left? How much real-life fun did they get?

Like me, they loved playing. Like me, lust was a flash of enjoyment and a moment of ecstasy. We are all screwed up. We are all pervs.

But who cares? Really. Because come tomorrow, there will always be more fish to catch.

THE BYEONTAE GAME

Their eyes widened, and their lips lifted into smirks. The Pervert Game. Those magic words worked wonders. Never once did any of the guys stop there. Everyone wanted to know.

"What is that game?" they all asked, "How do you play it?" And in between the lines, they wondered what they'd get for winning it.

Men were men. My first test had proven true.

And the second test was that age didn't matter. They wanted me. This felt good. A finger to the jerk boy who said Ajummas sucked. My naughty plan to corrupt Korean men's minds was on fire. The success rate was 95%, with only one out of fifty men saying no. He was happy not playing the game when he learned the rules. I took it as him being careful. True, the internet was flooded with scammers.

The Byeontae Game was a litmus test. A telling sign of the type of men I wanted to meet and gather the stories I sought, and the ultimate goal, if the vibe permitted, was to pound our brains out. Excuses were aplenty. Whatever the reason, the journey was a sexy thrill I couldn't get enough of.

This plot began a month prior.

I stumbled upon many YouTubers chatting and recording their conversations with strangers they met on OmeTV and Omegle. Two online random chat apps that matched you with strangers in your chosen countries provided language translation message boxes for those who don't speak the language.

The Korean strangers chatting with these YouTubers, who often pretended they couldn't speak Korean, were so intriguing that I kept returning for more. They were the real version of K guys I saw in my drama, and like many women brought in by the K-wave, I wanted to know more about this hot new species.

The everyday Korean guy.

I was on overdrive, wanting to meet such people and wondering if that was possible. And so the pre-game was hatched. I wrote my cheatsheets. The what-ifs and questions I wanted to ask were translated and sounded out so I could read off the papers and communicate.

Old school, yes. I should have pulled out a translation app, yes. In all my exuberance, I wasn't thinking straight. After many tries and setting up my fake accounts and VPN, I was ready and set to fire. And after the first shot down, it took days to climb back up.

And then one day, I logged in. A new guy's face popped up. I stared into his bedroom and then back at him.

"Annyeonghaseyo (안녕하세요)," he said. "Eodiseo osyeossnayo (어디서 오셨나요)?"

I jumped and slammed my laptop shut. My heart was racing at two hundred miles an hour. It took several more tries. Each time before clicking START, I took deep breaths for forty minutes, tried to calm down, and then freaked out again. Slowly, that time dropped to thirty minutes, then twenty, ten, and finally five minutes.

I wasn't usually an Introvert, but this strange communication method was past my playing field. Breaking out of my bubble was harder than I thought. Still, I was relentless and forced myself to small talk and break the silence, extending the cross-country conversations with the longest I'd spoken to at ten minutes.

And then, one night, with my cheat sheets in hand, I finally braced myself to ask my first Korean guy to play the Byeontae game. I picked an easy target — one with a chest, no face, no legs, and a high chance of a naked ass and penis in hand.

He wasn't my kind of fish because I wanted a face and a friend. But he was easy to catch and had a good first try.

"Annyeong," I said, and he waved and pointed down. I giggled. "What are you doing?"

The text box blinked, translating his Korean to mine. "Show me your boobs."

I was surprised at how bold he was. Most of the Koreans I spoke to beat around, and we never got past asking my question before we ended.

"Play the Byeontae Ajumma (변태 아주마) game with me," I said.

"Byeontae Ajumma?" He spoke aloud in surprise. "Pervert?"

"Yes!" I giggled, "Ten…" My voice shook. The hook was in, and I was reeling. "Ten questions!" I showed him both hands, fingers extended. "You five…" I dropped one hand and pointed at him.

He didn't have a face, but a thumbs-up meant he understood. I jabbed my finger on my zipped hoodie. Underneath was my secret weapon and final test.

"I five." I paused, letting the air in, and extending that pause, "If I like your questions and answers, I will show you my boobs."

There was a moment of silence.

I could almost hear his brain clicking, and the moment his

cock overruled. I couldn't have picked a better candidate, but his not speaking made me braver.

And then he raised his thumb.

I grinned. I couldn't help myself. It would be my first live erection, and I was beyond excited.

The text messages appeared again, "I can't speak English. Can I type?"

"Yes...but I hope they don't censor..." I bit my lip. I was kicked out twice before this for who-knew-what-reason. It was almost like the app knew I was up to no good. A pre-emptive measure to make me quit when I still could — that slippery slope. Once I got on, I knew there was no climbing back. After creating several accounts, emails, and whatnot, I was back in vid chatting.

I nodded hard, "Never mind. It's okay. I'll start first. What is your favorite sex position?"

I could see the words coming—the typing and then stopping.

"At the back. Hitting the ass," he replied.

"Doggy!" I bounced on the bed. "My favorite!" I giggled.

At that moment, My heart was light. He was a friendly pervert as I watched his thumb go up. I didn't ask where the other hand was. There wasn't a point in stating the obvious. "Your turn!"

"What size are your breasts?" he asked.

I giggled and jiggled my boobs hidden under my hoodie. "Size D."

"When is your first time?" I smiled. "Seventeen. Namja chingu. (남자 친구)." Most people's first love was their boyfriends or girlfriends. Stats were in the range of seventeen to early twenties.

The cursor started again. "Fifteen years old."

My jaw dropped.

"With the female teacher in the science lab room." The words appeared.

"Oh my god…" My jaw dropped. "OMG!" I typed and shouted. "Tell me more! Tell me more! Who started it first?"

He laughed. We both laughed. We connected right there.

This was what I wanted. Talking about sex broke language barriers. It brought strangers closer. We were like pals. No rules, no judgment.

"She did. I did." The message said. "She pulled me into the lab, pushed me into a chair, and sat on me. She wore a white shirt, a grey skirt, and no panties."

"Damn! That was so hot! Like a hentai manga!" I laughed and giggled. Forget the cheatsheet. The translations worked. This was gold. Yes. It was illegal. It was at least ten years ago; looking at him, he was definitely an adult.

No judgements.

"Show me your boobs." He asked again. "I want to cum."

"Show me," I smiled and pointed down. He made me brave. This was the first time for everything.

I heard him laugh, and his camera panned down. He was skin-tight, pink, and stiff. I watched, mesmerized by his hand moving up and down his shaft.

"I want to see your boobs," he said this time.

I could go on and insist on the five questions each, but what he gave was worth more than that. Slowly, I unzipped. The thrill of him watching sent shockwaves from my fingertips to my shoulders and down my back.

"I've never done this before…" I said as I watched his hand move faster as he jerked himself.

"Take off your shirt," I said.

I watched him pull his white shirt off and stare at his chest. He wasn't super muscled, but I liked it: pale, smooth skin and squared shoulders.

I stared down at my half-unzipped hoodie, revealing the curves of my large breasts. I zipped it off in a flash and pushed back the sides, squeezing my breasts.

He inhaled loudly.

"I want to see your pussy," he said.

"No," I said, zipping up.

"No. Open. Keep open."

"I showed you..." I stared at his chest, realizing I still didn't know what he looked like. "I think we're done."

"No! Wait..." He waved at me and started typing. "I'll answer more questions," he messaged.

And just as I was about to answer him, the screen skipped. My horny guy was gone, replaced with another face, and before I could react, the site shut down.

I was kicked out — banned, and I didn't get his contact. The guy with his fifteen-year-old virgin with his teacher story was gone, zapped into the dark pits of ones and zeros.

Later that day.

"Why are you so happy?" My hairdresser asked.

"Am I?" I smiled in the mirror.

"Yes, you're smiling a lot today. When you come and see me, you are usually tired."

She was right.

Why? Because I saw my first stranger cock, and I loved it.

HOW I MET MY SECOND HUSBAND

"**D**o you want to play Byeontae Game?"

I stared at the guy on the other side of my screen. His bedroom was simple, with a bed, table, monitor, and gaming chair.

Some guys had a shelf for books, collectibles, or a rack of clothes hanging on exposed rods. Most rooms were white or had wallpaper. A few had golden lights, pipes on the ceiling, an old-style home with shoji-like screens, or the sneaky ones — outdoors by a stairway, in a factory doing the night shift, in a park, or in his car.

This guy's table was scattered with books. From his disheveled hair and T-shirt, he looked to be in college.

Early twenties or mid if he'd gone to the army first, which was mandatory in Korea. His black mask covered half of his face. Like many guys on the video chat app, his eyes were bright, black, with sexy monoids.

The Byeontae Game (변태게임).

Yes, my first bait to the gateway of Korean guys. My goal is to prove two things and enjoy the third.

Korean guys aren't the romantic, chivalrous, innocent guys in Kdrama or Kpop. They are as normal guys as everyone else.

Milfs are popular anywhere. Mommies are universally loved and, to those perverts, worth the chase.

The most fun and challenging is pushing boundaries and corrupting more of those "innocent" Korean men's minds. How far can I push them and myself?

Tempting, seeing, tasting, smelling, and feeling. Passion, running deep as it grows inside my body and theirs, exploding into a million stars.

I am unapologetic. Objectification is a two-way street. They gained as I did, too. And in this game of play, society's rules are left at the door. There are no levels of speech and no age distinction.

The lion can be the lamb, and the young stud, the wolf.

I call it my social experiment.

"Stop giving excuses," H said. "You had an affair."

"It was online! Okay. I was wrong." I replied.

It took me four months to come to terms with it.

I am a hunter — a cougar by instinct. The thrill of capturing a fish, savoring their lust as they plunged into mine—mixing minds and liquids, fantasizing and escaping to greater heights, has always been my dream.

"What's a cougar?" Many of the guys ask. They are familiar with the Milf, but the mountain cat is alien.

A cougar is a woman in her forties who loves younger men at least ten years younger than her — the hot woman who gives guys a hard-on. Fit to a T, there is no denying who I am.

Sex is a drug—a high that leaves me in a drowsy state of languor. Guys like them are like lint to my fire, and I am there for them mentally, physically, and emotionally. An ear listening to their woes, a naughty angel, a passionate dream, a dirty slut who fed into their needs.

"Byeontae game?" His eyes widened, and his lips lifted shyly.

This was what always got me—it made my heart flutter hard as I watched this supposedly innocent young man turn into a wolf.

"How do you play?" He asked.

"Ten questions." I raised my hands. "Five you, five me. Sex questions…if I like them, I'll show you my boobs."

The rules were easy. No translations were needed. The universal language of sex sped through all doors. And big boobs were the international currency.

The first test passed. Korean men are also men.

Millions of women have fallen like dominoes to these Korean guys and still do, thinking these Cinderella men will be the perfect boyfriend and, with his parents' approval, his precious wife.

Kwave brought yellow fever. Korean tourism is on a high. Seoul is the mecca where dreams are dashed and reality sets in.

But for me, baby cougar, the hunt began from a random chat app, and so did those Hongdae boys. This sumo match was to see who got the upper hand.

Second test. Age was just a number.

A F-you finger to the jerk boy from another day, in another chat, who said, "Ajuumas suck!" His disgust only stoked the flames in me. My naughty plan to corrupt Korean men's minds was bon-firing.

Milfs were a real thing. Had I known earlier, I would have flaunted my assets — big boobs, big butt, small waist. BBSW.

Asian women weren't sexualized this way. We were taught since birth that body objectification was bad, and slimness was the standard.

Having surfed through this chat app and in my journey to this point, I've learned that Korean men, like all men, appreciate a wide range of body types. Curvy, succulent breasts and wide hips were just as popular as skins of every color. Kbeauty existed because human hangers made clothes beautiful.

Women didn't need to starve themselves. We are all gorgeous in our own way. It is time to free ourselves from the judging eyes of other women and small-minded men.

Venus wasn't a wraith. Mother Nature at her best was a Milf. She held the balls of men in her hands and helped seed the world with her lovers.

"Annyeonghaseyo," the college student said. "Eodiseo osyeossnayo?"

Two simple questions — Hi, and where are you from?

His smile and curiosity were enough to burst through my defenses. Here I was, wearing my sunglasses. A tight blue hoodie zipped over a black lingerie dress, and snuggled in lace were my prized boobies in size Ds.

We switched to a different chat app, and he said, "Let's play the game now."

"What's your favorite position?" I started first.

"Doggy," he said.

"Me too!" I grinned.

"When was your first time?" he asked.

"College," I said. "College," he replied.

"Where did you have the most exciting sex?" I asked.

"Stairway…now, show me your boobs," he said—a quick segue and to the point.

I unzipped slowly, letting my plump flesh fill in the space, dominoes of flesh.

He inhaled. I watched him reach down, his sneaky fingers and eyes never leaving my chest.

"How old?" He asked breathlessly. "Me, eighteen."

"Close, seventeen and a half," I replied. And then, my boobs sprang out with the sound of metal teeth unclasping, revealing my porcelain bouncy appendage.

He was in machine mode, jerking hard, already revealing his stick without shame.

I smiled. I couldn't help it. His excitement was mine. I breathed in his lust. I was drawn to him and wanted more.

"How about your pussy?" he asked in a raspy voice.

"Maybe?"

He showed me all of his shaft in three-sixty, and because I liked him, I gave in and showed him what he wanted, pulled out my dildo, and then it was on to the flash of hands, legs, mouth, private parts, and my toy.

Things moved fast and loud when emotions were high. I orgasmed and watched him ejaculate.

White and thick.

It was perfect timing, all I wanted. And that was how I met my 'Second Husband.'

Everyone has an origin story. Mine is funny, awkward, and sexy. Baby cougar taking her first steps as her cage creaked open. The world beyond the suburbs was rough, unfettered, and filled with digits of ones and zeros.

I could go anywhere I wanted with the touch of a keypad. Flash all I want, do naughty things with strangers, and bear no repercussions. Fire burning bright. Or so I thought.

I wasn't ready then. But the excitement was brewing — the thrill of doing things I'd never done before – meeting others in real life. We didn't have a hookup period. H and I were college sweethearts from Freshman Year.

And then three years ago, we decided to Yolo. To go Open, to date, and play with others.

This wasn't just in my mind. This could happen. The sex. It would be a boost in ego, skin-to-skin contact with a stranger, unrestrained fun, the flush of orgasm, and more.

They, the Koreans and other Asians overseas, think that we, being foreigners, are "Open-minded". No, Americans are not all "Open". This Yolo experience was a choice. Call it a midlife crisis, Carpe diem, Feminism, love thyself.

If not now, when?

If I don't love myself and be true to myself, when?

Talking about Sex opens all doors. Secrets spilled from every-day guys you'd never thought would.

This is real. Everyone has a story.

And these are my Confessions.

CHAPTER TWO

NAUGHTY AND NICE

MOMMY'S BOY

I am a Milf. Yes, the mommy whom guys love to fuck. Unlike the fakers who used #Milf on their porn to get hits, I am the real deal. Kids under my belt, a housewife dressed in lingerie, and a career woman who gave up promotion for her family.

> Milf by day, cougar by night. Fun-loving,
> kind, smart, and loves to laugh.
> Hotwife, looking for her pervert friend
> byeontae chingu 변태 친구.
> Fwb, Open-minded, and NSA,
> unless you wanna tie me up.
> [East Asian boys only.]

Adding to my dating profile some more tongue-in-cheek vibes and cute, sexy pics, funny snipes, and comments — that was how I worked it. Laying the bait to catch some yummy fish.

When I started, my highest score was more than ten thousand likes on Tinder in less than a month. The fish kept coming, but only a few made the type cut. And less would I chat with and point to my Insta, and from there, we'd have sexy fun.

They lapped it up. My pics and vids, and they gave their personal shares. If time permitted, I wanted to video sex because that was how I got my high and a guarantee they weren't some catfishes. And when summer came, I added my promise that maybe, just maybe, we could meet in Korea and seal the deal if we kept in touch and matched.

I never knew a Milf commanded such power. Empowered by my curves and the adoration of young men and their kinks, I was ready to catch me some fish.

"Mommy, how I love to fuck you." Some would say. "It is my dream to fuck a Milf." Others said.

Friend of my son, stepson, nephew, or a more sick imagination rolling in their heads. Childhood trauma? Maybe? Most likely. Something we chose to ignore because it was messy, grey, that would make this so wrong.

Guys, imagine this. You stepped into the house and saw me in my apron, moving around the kitchen, stirring at a pot and frying at the stove.

"Mommy," you said.

Delicious smells rising from my pots and pans while you crept in, wrapping your arms around my waist. I gasped at your tight-back hug and smiled. Your lips were planted on my neck as you breathed in my clean scent of body soap and the shampoo of freshly washed hair. My wavy curls tickled your nose, and my giggling and soft struggles made you grow hard. The lace and silk of my lingerie was like cool water running through your fingers.

You made me drop what I was holding, dragging me to the kitchen counter, and slapping my ass hard as you pushed me to face the table.

You fantasized about it often.

Sometimes you lifted my lingerie and greedily eyed my T-panty, slicing my ass cheeks into two equally large bites. You squeezed my large, tight butt and slammed your body, hip, groin, and legs against mine. Then, you made a sudden thrust, and I felt you in that motion.

I was trapped as you grabbed my arms behind my back — hot breath against my neck. You took a bite, and I moaned. You pushed down your pants, dick springing up, hard between my ass and stroking my thighs. A quick brush of skin to skin, and you entered, defiling me in the kitchen where children's mouths were fed — the holy shrine of family life.

It is kinky. Damn, my kind of byeontae because you're my type of guy. This is definitely on my list of acts I'd like to do repeatedly with the young fish I find.

Who doesn't like food and porn? Or better yet, food porn. Another idea that I loved, and also on my list of things to do.

But, the first guy who called me mommy rubbed me the wrong way. Despite being high on sexual fumes, that word was enough to bring me back to earth.

He was twenty-four, still in college in Southern California, and visiting Seoul. He was under my age range by a year — my sweet spot of twenty-five to thirty-five. I was new then. Anything younger, my guilt sat on my shoulder, nagging about rights and wrongs.

The devil was in disguise, with the gleeful laughter of H and the guys I knew. Egging me on to conquer the younger, the better. They have no problem fucking girls that young, so why shouldn't I do the same?

"So long as they are legal."

"They are adults. They know what they are doing."

"Do you think they don't fuck?"

"This is awesome! Now, you're a real Milf!"

"Hahaha...Mama's boy."

"Suck up those young men's energy!"

And damn, this guy, this twenty-four-year-old, was eye candy. Hard to resist. Easy enough to be one of those K-pop idols. Smooth-faced, with floppy hair over his beautiful almond eyes, tall, long-legged, and with defined chocolate abs and lean chest. The first thing he asked when we met on Ometv was if I was a Milf and what was with my shades.

Told him I couldn't trust the people on that app, and he said, as did everyone else, that I could trust him. Still, I kept my sunglasses on because the guy before him was just as cute, except he was hiding in a dark room, and I had suspiciously felt he was filming, which made me skip him with a flick of my fingers.

You would have thought I'd learned my lesson for the day, but the horniness was running in my veins, and I had to get those feelings out, or I'd never be able to walk out of the house without stripping every guy I saw.

He took his clothes off quickly as I did my flasher dance in black lace, stripping off layer by layer. His hand went to his pink erection as I pulled out my purple dildo and gave it a good lick and suck.

My saliva dripped down my rubber sword. He gasped as he watched my dildo go in and out of my mouth. My puppy-pink tongue was licking, swiping left and right.

"What is your favorite position?" I asked, my voice dropping low.

"Doggy. Cowgirl." He jerked hard. "You're a mom…you're a fucking mom. Slut!"

"Yeah," I winced. "Slut…I love sex," I pounded into my wet pussy.

"Fuck you! Fuck!" He moaned.

"Yeah…fuck," I grinned.

"I WISH I WERE YOUR SON, AND YOU BIRTHED ME, AND I'M FUCKING YOU!" His eyes rolled back. "FUCK YOU! I'LL FUCK YOU HARD! MAMA BITCH!"

"Whoa," I froze, jaw dropped, and my dildo rolling off my fingers.

This dude wanted me to be his real mom. Giving birth to him, and then he fucked her? Now, that was seriously messed up.

Fingers wet in my pussy juice. To say I was shocked was taking it lightly. He was going on, jerking away happily, mumbling those sinful words, not realizing that I'd stopped.

"What did you just say?" I said, lusty voice returning to normal. My mind fog cleared, and I felt weird. "You want me to be what?"

He stopped and finally opened his eyes. Those dilated black irises darted to me as if he were seeing me for the first time. "You birthed me…"

And my ears were still bleeding from the "wish I was your son and you birthed me and I'm fucking you" words. He had mommy issues, and my curiosity was piqued.

The dude was twenty-four, which makes him about two decades younger than me. But the devils were speaking in our ears as we assessed each other earlier. The sex thrill was too much to resist.

"What the hell?" he said.

When we first met, he asked how old I was, and I vaguely told him I was a cougar.

"I'm horny. I have a girlfriend," he said.

"I'm married," I told him.

"So?" He frowned.

Twenty minutes later, seconds after his revelation, we were still in the throes of vid sex, and I wondered if it was time to regret. But I'd already shown him everything to see, and that silver lining to my peak was within sight. Like him, I was horny, and my needs wanted to be met. Since when did I become so casual with sex and flashing my body as if I were taking a walk in the park? When did I arrive at this point?

"You don't like it?" He mustered a voice, still rubbing his dick, and I couldn't help but watch the fine body and that pumping motion — screw guilt.

"I'm not your mother," I said with that firm voice a mom would use. I hated myself for doing that. I watched him squirm but sensed the sexy danger racing through his suddenly bright eyes.

Damn. This guy had issues. And I had to because I was on a lust high and wanted that release.

"I know," he said, closing his eyes and hand jerking back hard; his cock was slapping. "You're not my mama. Is that okay? You're my mommy slut."

"Yes…I'm a slut. Bad slut," I said, falling back into character.

Terrible me. I'm letting this pass. All wrongs made right by this chance to fuck a guy like him. I'm a terrible person.

Whatever. The hunter was on. I was after my prize. Objectification was legit if both parties agreed to it. My fetish would be served.

"Bad, dirty mama. I'll fuck you bitch. Fuck you so hard, you'll cry for me."

"Sure. I'm a bad mama, but I'm not your mama," I replied, my voice taking a serious tone.

He laughed. "You're my bad bitch. Slap your ass. I wanna hear it." And so I did because slapping was my pain and pleasure, and as he laughed and commanded more, I complied because what was good for him was also good for me.

Each of us was riding high; the end was in sight. I watched him cum. Spraying gloops of white like a gurgling fountain. I cummed soon after, my body shaking off the ecstasy.

Beautiful.

We smiled and said our goodbyes. The boner was over, and I'd blocked him after, which I'm sure he did too. A one-time sin was more than enough.

—oo—

SHOT

—oo—

" **I** 'm going to shot now. In your mouth."

"I'm going to shot in your ass."

"I'm going to…"

It took me three times to realize it wasn't lost in translation. 'Shot' meant 'shoot', and in his terms, it meant ejaculate.

I dropped into a jungle where I didn't know the rules. These people, these Koreans, weren't like me. We might have the same skin color, but our different cultures run deep. This was also why they were an enigma.

"Is Byeontae bad?" That was one of the ten questions I asked when we began my Byeontae game. He was my first online sex friend and the reason why I cheated on H.

It was my first time dealing with a Fuckboy; too hot to resist. It was like having a Kpop star and chatting with him in person. His tattoo made it even harder to resist, and being new to the hunt, I didn't know what a Fuckboy meant until it was too late.

Too late because I'd fallen too deep, and my sins were too heavy to crawl out of the hole of my own making.

Curiosity killed the pussy cat. I thought I was smart. Creating a persona, a sexy game, and a world where I thought no one would know me.

I asked Fuckboy for his name. He said I didn't need to know. I thought he was trying to save me from lying, but later, I realized it was because he knew how to play the game better. Fucked her and dropped her.

I told him I was going to tell my husband. In all my naiveté, I knew what I had done was wrong and wanted to come clean. The thrill was exhilarating, but I always knew the consequences I had to bear.

"Why?" His voice dropped from his usual smoothness. "He doesn't need to know."

"Are you afraid he'd be mad?" I said.

"Of course…don't tell him." This was after our session of fun. He told me what to do and the positions he wanted me in as he shook his hard stick and pumped it as I thrusted my dildo into mine.

"I want to," I said.

"I don't think it is a good idea…"

"Doesn't matter. I don't like keeping secrets from him."

I had my fun and knew I had to pay the price. Our marriage would face this test. I won't deny I played with a stranger online. I cheated on my husband because the allure of something hot and different was too much to resist. Over the twenty years, I hid who I was, and the truth was breaking out.

I was a Succubus.

Forced into hiding and forced to face the reality of living. Earning our keep, getting the residency card I needed to stay in this country, not of my birth. To start a family and build that family up. The lives of others were constantly placed before mine.

For once, I wanted to be selfish. To do something I wanted, to be happy for myself.

"I played with a Korean guy online," I confessed. "We did it, five times vid chat."

"I'm disappointed," H said after taking a while to digest.

"You're not angry?" I asked.

"I'm sad you did it, but I know why…"

H and I spent the whole week after my confession talking. We decided to try an Open relationship after.

Three years later, here we were, adjusted and settled into our new alternate lifestyle. The initial road was bumpy as hell. The rules were unclear and written in tears, but a few things became clear.

I was a Hotwife, and a Milf Cougar.

"No. Byeontae is okay," Fuckboy replied. "But Korean girls don't show their byeontae side because of our culture."

Yes, I was different from these girls. Or maybe they were just better at hiding it.

"Do you see girls here?" I asked one of the guys I met on Ometv.

"Yes. I chatted with them. Korean girls," He replied.

"Really?"

My hunt was on. Pretending to be a guy and hiding in the scenes like some of them do. Finding those elusive Korean girls and wanting to ask them if they'd play my Byeontae game with me.

I didn't like girls sexually, but I'm curious what they thought.

How shy were they about sex? I wanted to prove Korean guys were as normal as any guy anywhere. Those Korean girls couldn't be those shy, silly, innocent women that drama portrayed.

Okay, I admit. Corruption was the goal. I was ready to turn everyone into horn dogs and bitches. Sex made us Open. To face who we were.

And I found them — those few girls. Many skipped me when I popped my head out and revealed I wasn't a guy. I met two Korean girls who stayed to talk.

One was an innocent-looking girl who seemed fresh out of or still in high school. The mommy in me told her to get off this app. Though Korean, she was from Uzbekistan and only spoke Uzbek and English. Such a cute girl, and before we could get into deep talks, the screen skipped.

The second girl I met blew smokes in circles. We made plans to meet offline on Insta, but she ghosted me, as many did, soon after. Ghosting fucking sucked, and my bruised heart kept going.

One, two, three shot

The percentage of horn dogs with shaking dicks on Ometv was 50:50.

"You don't want to be here. There are many dirty guys here," said one kind soul.

"Oh, really?" I smiled with my shades on. Initially, this virtual chat app was my go-to haunt. I was fishing about two to three times a week, with one to two guys a day, and orgasming once, twice, or even thrice. The numbers were insane, and at some point, I stopped keeping track of them virtually.

This was good practice. I had my performance down, and I was in a perpetual high. I was shedding my shyness, building my fetish, flashing my body in the light of day. I was embracing the truth of who I was.

Sucking the youth. At that time, my range was 25-35 years old. Eating them online. Slurping the essence as we imagined doing it in real life. Cumming separately, cumming together, and doing the dance of virtual sex.

"Why? What's wrong?" I asked one time when I was orgasming to a guy watching. He was jerking off as far as I could tell with his hand below the screen. His face was pained.

"Where are you going?" I asked.

The screen turned black, and I heard his scrambling in the background.

"Hello?" I stopped and pulled my dildo out, waiting and panting after my performance.

A text came after. "I underestimated the power of vid sex."

"What do you mean?" I texted back.

"I had to go to the toilet and cummed so hard," he replied.

I laughed so hard my sides hurt. "You should have shown me. I love watching men cum."

"It's my first time online…" he said.

Though I couldn't see him, I felt his embarrassment.

"It was fun, wasn't it?" I asked.

"Yeah," he replied.

I was proud of deflowering their virtual experience — the power of owning another and showing the innocent guys this amazing high.

"Why are you wearing sunglasses?" he asked.

Back to the kind soul on Ometv. He was a handsome guy with brown hair tinted a shade darker. A story about him would come later.

"Because I don't want to be recorded," I said, studying him behind his hand, hiding part of his face.

"Why would anyone record you?" He tilted his head.

I laughed. Giggled hard with my hand over my mouth.

Because, even with cool shades on, no one knew. In my zipped hoodie and friendly face, I was a contradiction. Under my hoodie, I wore black laced lingerie, heavy breasts perked, ready to play. Outside, I was just a normal mom.

"Do you want to play a Byeontae game?" I asked. Forget Korean. Sex spoke all languages, and big boobies were the currency exchanged.

Fun was just a zip away. The horny tank had to be filled for today. Fishes came, and fishes go.

One, two, three shot. Watching him squirt. Thick and white, just the way I liked it.

—oo—

YOU

—oo—

He was the fish that got away. The kind soul who would have been a great buddy or Fwb.

"I know I'm going to remember you forever after tonight," he said. "I won't forget you, my sweet Byeontae Ajumma."

When he said that, I thought he was being nice. Had I known he'd planned never to contact me after his confession, I'd worked harder to keep him close. He would have been perfect for my harem — a fish worth keeping and feeding.

I regretted it. To this day, three years later, I regret not doing the things I should have done with him that I so carelessly gave away to other guys who meant nothing to me. It was strange how chemistry worked. It wasn't so much that I was attracted to him, but I missed more of the camaraderie.

He, whom I called 'Buddy', could have been a good friend. We shared the same jokes, talked about the same sexy stuff, and had the feels for the stories that bothered us. And we spoke for 2.5 hours and could have gone on if he wasn't so tired, and it was already 4 a.m. in the morning.

It began like this — the screen flipped. My heart pounded as I waited for the room to clear and for the next person in the window to appear.

He was lying on his bed. I checked the time on my phone. It was two a.m. there in Korea. White blinds were pulled down, and his bed was like many others I'd seen many times before. I remembered white sheets, a window with drawn-down blinds, and his light brown hair. His hand was on his face because he wasn't wearing a mask.

"Hello," I said.

"Where are you from?" He said immediately in English. There wasn't a Korean accent. He could easily be any guy from here.

"US, California," I replied.

"What are you doing here?" He sounded bored and tired.

"Meeting new people," I replied.

"Why are you wearing sunglasses?"

"Why are you covering your face?" I grinned.

"There are stalkers here."

"There are? How? Everything is random." I replied to the way the system worked. You never know who you're gonna get, and with my VPN, the screen flipped suddenly, and the new 'friend' whom I'd just made would be gone forever into the abyss with the 51.7 million Koreans whom I'd never know. Because of that, I'd give my Insta almost instantly if the guy seemed good. It's better to hook first and check later.

"Have you watched the show, 'YOU'?" He asked, sitting up on his bed. The screen of his mobile phone showed the bottom of his lip.

This guy was cautious.

"Yes, that psycho serial killer," I answered.

"This is my advice. You need to protect yourself." He combed his brown, wavy hair with one hand.

"Okay…?" I answered, intrigued that I got someone interesting.

On a Saturday morning with nothing much to do, my kids were playing their video mobile games, and I was alone in my room, feeling horny and searching for the next bite.

"There are a lot of creepy people here. Creepy men who you don't know what they are thinking. They can stalk you like that man on the TV," he said.

"That's messed up. Very creepy..." I nodded, excited that I was talking about something more than basic.

This guy had potential. I could see Fwb written all over his face if only he'd show me his face. I'm not a face person, but my guy has to be easy on the eye, and I'd like to know who I was dealing with. "Psycho thriller, serial murder...crazy."

"Yeah..." He leaned back into his bed headrest.

"I'm a writer, an author," I smiled.

"Really?" He was happily surprised.

"Yeah." I nodded. "Not as creepy a story as 'You'. Not sure if it'd be popular. Anyways," I sighed. "So why are you talking about creeps?"

"Many people show their sausages here." His voice lowered into confession as if he was protecting me from the seedy nature of this app. What he didn't know was that he was dealing with a hunter — a cougar who loved the sight of jerking off. In fact, that was her all-time fav fetish.

This was always the paradox of who I am. By appearance, I was the nice, sweet, and cute mama. No one ever thought I'd be this dirty perv with roaming hands. Eyes that dropped to every man's crotch she passed. My mind fixated on the next imagination of sex.

"Oh...really? I think I saw less than ten." Inside, I was laughing, snickering like a teenager hooked on a secret the adults didn't know.

"Why are you smiling?" He dropped his hand, and I saw his face.

My mouth dropped. I hurriedly cover it. My heart lurched.

Damn, he was hot. As hot as one of those Kdrama actors. But I didn't want to appear ditzy, so I tried to keep my cool. He had big brown eyes like a puppy. A friendly face, boyish handsome.

"Take off your sunglasses." He smiled.

"I…"

"I'm showing you my face. Your turn."

"I'm married. My husband made me promise to keep it on."

"Oh, you're married? You sound young and looks, well, I can't see your face," he said.

I took off my sunglasses and then covered the bottom half of my face with my hand.

"You're cute." He smiled. "Take off your hand."

I felt my ears heat up. I figured it was too late. He saw my face when I took off my sunglasses.

I blushed again and dropped the hand. "Thanks…so why are you on Ometv?"

He scooted back down in his bed and dropped his head on his pillow. "I was watching the game (World Cup) and couldn't sleep after. It's the weekend, so I don't care. If tomorrow is Monday, I'd have to sleep."

"I see…" I adjusted my black lingerie under my blue hoodie, suddenly feeling guilty about wearing my hunter garb. This guy was too nice to be a perv. In fact, it would be nice to have a simple conversation.

"So?" He looked up. "Why are you here?"

I cleared my throat. This was the truth or lies moment. "Have you been stalked before?"

He nodded. "My ex was stalking me. She hacked my Insta and posted her pics on it and read all my messages."

"Oh my god…good thing you broke off," I said.

"I was in an abusive relationship…"

"Whhhaaat? You were? How?" It was hard to imagine that someone so hot like him would have to take crap from any girl or anyone.

"She'd scold me and hit me."

"What did she say?"

"Words to put me down so I'd feel like crap…"

"And hit you?" I asked. "I'm sure you're bigger than her."

"She'd flick her finger like this…" He showed me the finger flick game the Koreans like to play on their foreheads.

"What the hell? What the hell is wrong with her?" I cursed more. "And you dropped her fast, I hope."

"But sex was good. She liked to do it outside. One time, we did it behind a wall, and she got grass in her. I won't suggest that…"

"Wow…she's a wild one!"

"But…" He lowered his voice and looked away from my eyes. "This is embarrassing…she flicks my face, shoulders, penis, and balls. She was unstable…" he sighed.

"She threatened to kill herself…I was worried about confronting her because she might kill me and then herself. But, in the end, I did it. I told her. When we broke off, I closed my SNS down."

The world is full of crazy people. "You got away. That's all that matters," I said.

"And, I have a secret," he said.

"You can tell me," I replied.

"I filmed myself masturbating, and someone took my video," he said.

"Okay…" In this day and age, it was no biggie. I was sharing my sex vids with strangers, with no face.

"It had my face on it…" He looked pained.

"Oh shoot, I'm sorry to hear that…and what did you do?"

"I tried searching for it to get it pulled down, but I can't find it. I'm worried that someone I know has seen it."

Yes, that really sucks. Sex vids on the internet happen.

He messed his hair with his hands, looking even cuter and hotter.

"I wish no one you know sees it. But, if it happens, just say it was done without your permission."

"At least it is not a sex tape," I said.

"A sex tape is better, it is with someone. Better than jerking off alone…" He looked so sad. I can't do this to my family, I thought of killing myself."

"Oh my god! Don't! Your life is more precious than that stupid vid." I said that because I didn't understand the societal repercussions. I said words to tell him it was okay because to me, a life was way more important.

"Your family loves you more than that embarrassment. If you die, there is no turning back. It is done, you just have to move on. If you die, you will leave behind the hurts and scars in your family's heart, and that is way worse. Don't do it. You have to promise me."

He looked so sad. Depressed.

"I'm serious. You are important. People make mistakes. We are not all perfect. Yes, it really sucks. It is done. You have to love yourself, okay?"

He nodded. "Thanks for talking to me."

"Of course. We don't know each other, but I care. Just like you left that terrible ex, you can move on with this. Don't worry about it. If it appears, you have to brush it off and just say, "It was a mistake, I'm sorry. I won't do it again."

"A man doesn't run. A man faces the mistakes," I told him.

Man, woman, whoever. We are responsible for our actions, and lessons are meant to be learned. We grow as people for good or bad.

"If I could, I would reach over and hug you. You will be okay." He smiled.

"So why are you on Ometv?" He asked again. Maybe he was wondering why the zipper on my hoodie was low, or maybe he caught the swell of my boobs and black lace.

Guys didn't come to Ometv to find friends. Buddy was ready to have fun like I was. I remember saying to Buddy when he told me his naughty stories and that he was also byeontae, and I didn't believe him.

"Nah...you byeontae?" I said, shaking my head and squinting in disbelief. "You? You can't be byeontae..."

"Maybe not as much as you." He smiled. It was a nice, reassuring smile, a little goofy, and didn't seem to have any bad intentions.

"Yah. I'm really byeontae." I laughed. I saw myself on the screen. I came closer to my screen than I did with the rest of the men because we'd been talking for an hour about all sorts of things, and I'd decided I didn't have to seduce him, and this conversation was going to stay PG till he left.

Then I thought we were running out of things to say, and I felt that if I didn't complete my mission with this one, I would be betraying my initial intention. Besides, he didn't have Insta, and he had a bad experience with his stalker-ex, so the chances of him contacting me after were close to zero.

"Okay...there's something I need to tell you," I said.

"What?"

"Okay...I'm really nervous." I covered my face. My cheeks were heating up, and I couldn't really think of what was best to say. Besides, I'm terrible at comebacks. I'm not quick on my feet.

"Say it. You don't have to be shy. Just say it."

"I...I..." I sighed and closed my eyes. "I..."

"What?" He came closer to the screen as well. He might have coaxed me a few more times as I buried my head in my pillow. If it were anyone else, I wouldn't have struggled. In my mind, this guy was a good guy. We had a fun conversation, and I was going to blow it.

"Okay...you might hate me after this. I'm going to spoil this..." I pointed at him and me.

"Don't worry. It's really late. (3 a.m. Seoul time) I won't remember much. I'll forget it by morning. I always forget everything by morning."

"I came to Ometv to fish," I muttered quickly.

"You came to what?" He asked. "Can you speak louder? I won't judge. I don't judge people."

I took a deep breath. "I came to Ometv to fish. To find fuck buddies."

"Wow." He said and leaned back in his bed. "You did? Fuck buddies?"

I nodded, smirking now.

"You're married." He didn't push for my age earlier, and I didn't ask him his. I only knew he worked at an Interior Design firm and was studying journalism before that career switch.

"Yes," I said, smiling more.

He was smiling now. "So?"

"I'd ask them if they want to play a game."

"What kind of game?" He asked, grinning.

"Byeontae Ajumma," I said, more confident and proud.

"Ah. So did they play? What do you do?"

So, I told him my rules. He listened well. I could have easily led this conversation to asking if he wanted to play, but I wasn't sure what kind of signals he was giving.

"I'm feeling hot. Are you?" He asked.

It was January. The air was chilly, and the heater was on. "I'm okay." Baby cougar clueless.

"How do you do it with Number Two. Tell me step by step," he asked.

I should have caught on. Maybe it was then he grew horny, or when I pulled out my purple dildo to replay what I did with gestures.

In between our laughter at our/my antics and the experiences I had with those men, he might have wanted me to show him my boobs, too?

He called me 'Sweet Byeontae Ajumma,' and that was apt. We spoke for two hours till it was four-thirty a.m. his time, and he was really tired and had to sleep.

We shared the same wavelength, alike in so many ways. Frankly, it didn't matter how he looked or if he was a she. It was just the feeling of not having to pretend to be someone I wasn't.

"I will remember this night. I will remember talking to you in a long time from now," he said. "I won't forget you."

I should have told him that, too. And gave him another way

to be in touch. Forgot he didn't have Insta. Regrets are easier after the fact.

I searched for Buddy over and over again, month after month. Wanting desperately to replay what we didn't finish, worrying about his state of mind.

Dying is permanent, no repeats.

Let this book be viral. And, Buddy, if you see this. I hope you are happy wherever you are in Korea. And wherever you are, don't jump because I remember you.

—oo—

HAPPY ENDINGS

—oo—

Leave the Forever After to our books and TVs. That being said, anyone can get a Happy Ending. You just need to look hard enough.

Pay the right amount, and you can get that short bliss at your local Asian massage parlor. Just look for the business signboards that show 'feet' or one of those stores with the white curtains drawn out, sandwiched between an Asian restaurant and some other shop in a strip mall.

Yeah. If you're in the US, you know what I mean. Strip Malls are everywhere, and no, they are not Stripper's Mall. Just normal places with unnamed shops, small restaurants, and shops selling big refillable water bottles, kids martial arts, art classes, the local Kumon, or the laundromat, you get the gist.

To think, as you're walking by to your shop, that behind those curtains is a man lying on a massage bed naked except for a tiny piece of cloth on his body, and an older lady jerking him off.

His face is scrunched, and he is moaning. Getting there. His body is stiff and tingling. The rhythmic movements of her experienced, oiled hands added waves to his senses. His eyes closed because he is imagining a hot Milf masturbating him, and when he feels a wet mouth on his hard stick, that amazing, hot Asian mature woman with the big, juicy boobs and naughty mouth takes him in. Deep throating as he groans, feeling the need to burst.

He wants to hold back. To savor the moment longer. It was a

long while since he had a woman touch him. Those wet lips grip him tight. Warm, smooth hands trailing up and down the thin veins of his stiff rod.

He paid good money for this experience. Seeing the Ajumma is a disappointment, but who cares? With his eyes closed, she could be any female he wanted her to be.

"I'm coming…I'm coming…" He groans, his body spazzing as he spills his cum, like a fountain seeping from her fingers down her hands.

"Happy Ending good?" she asks. Totally ruining the moment. He nods, trying to hold on to the feeling a little longer.

She walks out of the room. There he is left naked with a towel over his chest, his limp, wet member exposed, and shamed.

When did he come to this point? That's when the present hits.

"Hi," he said.

"Annyeonghaseyo!" I replied. He was the first Korean stranger I spoke to outside my social circles. A man from the cheating dating app - Ashley Madison (AM). A man who was married.

"Nice to meet you. I'm K. Are you new here?" he asked.

"Yes. I started a few days ago." I replied. I won't bore you with the casual chats and how we got to the point where he was telling me his conquests on Insta.

K loved to talk. He loved talking most about the number of women he took. "My body count is high. A hundred," he said proudly.

"A hundred?" H laughed. At that time, H and I were just starting our Yolo experience. Our wings were wet, and H was my site admin on AM and monitored all my chats, and the sleazy ones that didn't pass my type profile. "It's obvious he's lying."

"It's possible to have slept with a hundred over several years. I mean, in ten years of sleeping around, it's very possible," I said.

"Sure. But a hundred? Why not a hundred-fifty-five, or ninety-seven? One hundred is too convenient a count. He wants you to think he's a great lover."

"Okay...," I said. H had a point. Guess I was too naive to think too much when I gave K the 'wow emoji'. Frankly, emojis were easy to give. Reactions didn't really mean anything online.

"How do you find the women?" I asked K. "Do you pay on Ashley?"

"I do," K replied. "It's easier to find a married or single woman on Ashley than on Tinder."

"What do you mean?" I asked. "Tinder is the best place to hook up."

"For the younger people. Ashley has more horny, desperate women."

What he also meant, which at that time I didn't know, was about odds.

Women ruled everywhere on dating apps. The proportion of single horny men was at least ten times higher than that of women. Normal, average, and below average women stood a better chance of leveling up. Of course, there were cases where hot men were just out for a quick fling and would say anything to get her to bed.

Sweet words, empty promises, ghosting, and flaking out. Those were words and actions I had to learn along the way.

"People online aren't real. You can't treat them as humans," said a friend. Every time I got hurt and I recalled his words.

"You can't be so naive and thin-skinned about this. You want to play, you need a thicker skin."

Yes, good sound advice. I admit, after falling and picking myself back up again, I was getting harder.

I do want to play. I do want to flirt, tease, use it, and lose it.

"Or I'd go to the coffee shop or laundromat. Those are good places to find horny women," K said.

Yes. Dear K was a man whore. He'd fuck anything with a hole. That explained his hundred lies. He told me about the hotel app where you can book a nice room for 70% off and cancel at any time. It was god-sent. A great way to save some money in the US, which didn't have those love motels like Japan, Korea, and all the other East Asian countries did.

Later, I learnt K was mid-ranking at a famous electric car company, which was fun because I'd tease him by sending nude pics of myself while he was at a meeting, especially when he was leading one.

One time, I sent a boob pic with a dildo on it. "Meet me now," I said. We'd been vid sexting, and the carrot was in.

"I'm coming!" he texted back, and from his panting later, he ran from his meeting room, across the hall of cubicles, past his colleagues, who thought he had a family emergency, and to his car, where he called me.

"I'd never done this before," he said. "This is crazy. You're such a bad girl," he laughed.

But he wasn't my type. He was in his late thirties, unlike the sweet twenties spot I'd begin to love.

Still, he was the first Korean guy I'd talked to and had many sexy stories to tell. The best was his 'Happy Ending' stories.

"I bought a monthly pack. It was just after military service in Korea, in my early twenties, when I got back to the US to work. One time, my back was hurting badly, so I asked my workmates where I could get cheap massages, and they were giving me strange looks and told me to go ask this guy in another department."

"When I went to the place, I was a little worried. It was located in a strip mall, in a somewhat run-down area. There wasn't a lobby; just some old wooden chairs and Asian-looking pictures on the walls, dated and patterned curtains pulled in. A flowery incense smell and an Asian lady, petite, about fifties, standing at a podium with a book," he said.

"Didn't you think it was suspicious? Why didn't you leave?" I asked.

"My back was hurting, and it was a good deal. Four massages for forty bucks. And that colleague swore they knew what they were doing."

Typical Asian. Who could resist a good deal? Those 'Buy one get one' offers, we loved them. Boast all day about them. Except in his case, he'd probably kept it to himself till he met me.

"I've not told anyone about this…," he said. "She led me to a room with a massage table. There was a hole in the middle of it."

OMG.

"I asked her what the hole was for and she said, 'To breathe'," he said.

OMG.

"She told me to take all my clothes off, and I asked if I could keep my underpants on," he said

"She said no."

Duh, of course.

"She gave me a small white towel, and I couldn't decide if I should use it to cover my ass or my penis," he said.

"So what did you do?" I asked.

"Jumped quickly on the table. She came in too fast. I covered my penis and lay on my stomach."

"And?" At this point, I'm laughing too hard.

"She was good. Her hands had good pressure, and my back was feeling less tight. Then, she told me to turn around."

OMG.

"The towel fell..." He paused.

"And then?" I asked.

"I was so embarrassed..."

"And...?"

"She pointed at my erection. It was semi-hard. You know, her touch was good...she pointed at it and asked if I wanted a massage. It's an extra charge."

"Ah, of course. So you said yes," I said.

"Well...yes...I mean, I haven't had a woman's touch."

"Dude. No judgments," I said. I was laughing till my cheeks hurt.

"And when she was massaging with the oils. She asked if I wanted a 'Happy Ending'."

At this point, I was a little clueless. "What's Happy Ending?" I asked an online friend.

"He got a 'Happy Ending'? Whoa. This guy. He's really desperate. What do you think it is?"

"Oh.my.god," I said. "They do that? But she's an older lady."

"Come on. Not that old...," said my online friend.

True. She wasn't that old. But she wasn't a hot woman. Guess it didn't matter.

"How was it?" I asked K.

"It was good. But I felt sick after."

Of course, he did. He had his Hyeonja Time, and feeling guilt seeped through his little guy up to his head. At least she got paid.

"Did you do it again?" I had to ask.

He gave me some naughty emojis. "My back was feeling better."

In his other tales, she gave him a nice prostate massage. Who cared how she looked?

Shy at first and then broken. The love for the handjob, blowjob, and Happy Endings.

Blowjobs. It seemed that was the common factor in all my chats and talks. The Milf was the experienced lover. The one who could give the best bjs and make him cum when his girlfriend or young wife could not.

And rumors and myths were true.

It was nature's calling, the pairing of young with old — the mature woman with the young man, teaching him the ways of the world, and the young girls and their sugar daddies, padding their purses, and gifting designer brands.

A Korean boy, D, who once had me ask if he should try one of those 'Happy Endings' places.

"My friend said it was so fucking good. Damn. He cummed so much. Had two women massaging his balls and taking turns to suck him," D said. "Do you think I should try?"

I rolled my eyes. Wtf.

"Dude. How did those women look?" I asked.

"Old? Maybe fifties. Asian. Low mid? He said one looked in her sixties!" D answered.

"And why do you need them?" I was feeling beyond annoyed.

"Hahaha…I guess I don't need one. I've a hot Milf like you. Told him that, and he was so jealous."

"Yeah," I replied — another man-boy. I seemed to attract these types often. In just those words, in my mind and in my books, I'd written him off.

Bugs who didn't know which was honey didn't get honey.

If Happy Endings were all a guy wanted. Red flags salute. He might as well stick his cock in a vacuum. Men could be dumb jerks, and Happy Endings didn't always end well.

It was unreal. Like looking into a dollhouse and watching, laughing along with the antics of someone who looked just like me. It had been months since the Yolo-ing, and I'd played the Byeontae game over and over again, and life was distinctively different from before.

"What have you been doing lately?" Asked a Mom friend. Mom friend is my kid's friend's mom, whom I hang out with because our kids are friends. "Why are you always so busy and have no time for coffee?"

Yeah. Coffee. How many times have I told them I didn't want to talk about kids? How many times did we have to talk in circles about inconsequential things that I didn't care for? I know it sounds rude, but my life was flashing by, and in the snap of a finger, all of this could be gone. And then what?

What do I have to look back on? Have I done everything I wanted to do or didn't know I wanted to do until it is too late?

"I want to go to a club," I told a friend.

"Why? It's not a big deal. Why are you so hung up about it?" He asked.

"Because I've not done it. I've not danced in a club or drank till I got drunk. Or been to a music concert?"

At that time, I had not. But since I made those requests after we went Yolo, I finally attended my first outdoor music concert and was surrounded by a crowd of 10,000 people at a Doechii concert. It was pure madness. The pungent stench of weed, the bodies of people squashing my personal space, and I was barely tall enough to see over their armpits.

Minutes later, I wanted out. The fear of being trampled on and night growing darker as cold seeped into my bones.

"Get me out! Get me out now, please..." I begged the guy I was with.

"You wanted to be here. This is what a music concert is. The crowd," he said.

Yes. It was. I was gonna die here.

The stampede in Itaewon on Halloween. This was not how I wanted to go. I still had many things I wanted to do. Many young guys I wanted to screw. I still had that Big Bang and the threesome and the many sexy games I wanted to play.

Would I do it again? No. But was it worth it? Yes. It was worth absorbing the vibe. Every bit of experience was exhilarating. No regrets.

The Byeontae Game was my first naughty game and that started my questions, and surveys on how guys think.

The men were opening up immediately. The game made us more comfortable with each other than we had ever been with anyone else. Secrets came pouring out, and yes, the orgasms and cums were deliriously fun, but it was also confiding with someone else across the world.

"Everyone has some screwed-up stories. This experience has taught me that women are just as dirty-minded as we guys, and if even a small percentage of women were like you, all of us would be the same," said a guy.

True. Behind those curtains, each family had its own problems, worries, and secrets no one knew.

Language was never the issue. Sex was just the start to something deeper. Yes, there were hungry, horny men, but there were also women like men, seeking more to life than a feeling of emptiness in their nest or wanting a brief moment of mindless happiness.

The months had taught me self-love. It gave me the confidence to open up and be who I am. As the road went on, the path was riddled with rocks, and I made mistakes. Finding the right line to draw in this perilous bog to who-knew-where was a challenge.

"You're always so impulsive." I've been told time and again.

True. I'm far from a saint. I had my flaws. This is the journey that I needed to be selfish. To grow to be the sexy, rude, confident goddess I am now.

I love sex, and so do they — those twenty-something-year-old men who piqued my curiosity.

Nothing to be shy about, because we are all adults here. And, I stand proud and say, this is who I am.

CHAPTER THREE

FULL SPEED AHEAD

—oo—

OILY LOLLY

—oo—

He was hard, shiny, and purple-pink.

Oiled from the tip of its head to the base of his balls. Taller than his hand and cleanly shaven like a magic staff held by a skilled wizard with nefarious plans.

I couldn't help but stare.

It wasn't just the shining monolith that caught my eye; it was the sound. The squeaky, squishy, jerky movements caught my attention.

He laughed because he knew he had me by my balls, which I didn't have, or I won't be watching the preview of his seductive cobra dance right then.

As I watched him go up and down, I wondered what made him do this. So openly displaying his shaft in shiny lolly-ness to anyone who stumbled into his room.

Ometv, the random chat app, made this possible. Revealing secrets of a stranger's life, daring them to show a part of themselves they usually wouldn't do.

The masks were off, and so were the clothes. There was a bravado and a false sense of security that no one would catch them, and what happened in Ome stayed in Ome. That was until some YouTuber or Influencer decided to film and blast our naughty deeds to the world secretly.

I swallowed hard. This must be how men felt. The tables were turned; instead of watching me as my dildo plummeted into my fair flesh, he was teasing me.

Other than the cock and facelessness, everything else in the room could be any other. Black shirt and black track pants — the uniform for most of the Korean guy population. His physique was lean with broad shoulders. Sitting on a comfy roller chair with a game computer on a desk. Most guys didn't show their beds until we moved to another social media app and started stripping.

He had a sexy baritone voice and a nice Adam's apple. There was a cheekiness to him with a whole lot of daddy, and that was how he got under my skin.

"Take off that hoodie," he said as his hand kept moving, thrusting in a smooth rhythm.

I was a mindless robot, slowly slipping off my black robe. Just days ago, I was pissed about Shot guy who stood me up again after learning that I told H about him.

Liquid slid down his shaft, glistening. Was it pre-cum? Why was the sound so musically delicious to my ears?

There wasn't a doubt I was a perv. A thirsty, horny Milf cougar who wanted nothing better than stepping into the screen and grabbing that alluring stick. I could imagine it, hard and oily, smooth and velvety, warm in my palm.

"I want to see your boobs," he said. Words that were said to another female would be harassment, but for me, it became an everyday language.

Slowly, I slipped off my laced black lingerie. My pearl-colored breasts bounced as they were freed from the strings that held them.

This was supposed to be my game. It was supposed to be revenge against Shot guy because I felt like shit for being ghosted.

However, this play of power with Oily Lolly switched with a simple act of jerking off.

"You want to suck it?" Oily laughed.

"What kind of oil do you use?"

"My secret?" Oily's voice held a grin.

Yes. What was that oil? Where can I buy some for my play?

The whole year and a half taught me a lot about what I liked, and what my type was. My husband was my type. Adding to our personalities, common likes and dislikes, those were reasons why we got along so well and never felt like we needed anyone else.

We were college sweethearts.

Was it common to last this long? It felt these days the divorce rate was 1 in 3. Twenty-five over years of loyalty and having one guy for the rest of my life seemed just fine until recently.

You only live once. Yolo. The fire inside me was burning. It didn't want to go gentle into that good night.

"Maybe everyone should try to be in an Open relationship before divorcing. Instead of cheating, being Open is better," someone said when he learned about my Open relationship. He didn't want to marry. In fact, many of the young guys and even those in their early thirties said marriage wasn't in their cards.

The world is changing every day. The new generation have different views on life and what makes them happy.

Coming out as Open wasn't a bed of roses. The start was awkward and hard for both of us. There was a lot of counting of the people I "scored" online.

True, I had ten thousand likes on Tinder in less than three weeks and thousands and thousands in all the other apps, but as I told him, those were quantity versus quality.

We went our own roads and build our contacts the way we liked. The journeys and stories were different. We were growing – apart and together.

And back to Mr. Oily Lolly. I did the usual pony trick. Squeezing my boobs, rubbing one after the other. Running my fingers over my nips and pinching them as they fell back with a bounce.

"More." His voice was husky now. His hand moved faster up and down his shaft. "Show me your wet pussy."

"I don't like to show you here. The VPN might skip. Do you have an Insta?"

He chuckled again. "I don't play Insta. Show it here."

This guy wasn't like the rest. A pity he hid his face, but so did I; that was the promise I made to H if I wanted to play on this app.

"You like it?" I asked after succumbing to his orders. A brat could only play as much as Daddy liked.

"Show me more." He growled, pumping harder, the squeaking noise ramping up.

"Like this?" I moaned, putting my fingers on my clit and rubbing them hard.

"Put your fingers in." The squishing sound was music to my ears.

"How about this?" I pulled out my dildo and stuffed it in. I groaned and moaned loudly. Our virtual act was getting hot. Super hot.

"Yes. I want to fuck you, you dirty slut." He groaned back.

"Yes, I'm a dirty slut. I'm your dirty slut."

This went on, him saying those words, and I repeating them — a chant, building up and ready to explode.

"Can I cum now?" he asked.

"Yes," I said.

"Who's my dirty slut?" he shouted.

"I'm your slut!" I hammered in.

And together, geysers ready to go, we exploded.

—oo—

FURBALLS

—oo—

He was stroking his cock in a Fursuit.

A cut-out hole just enough for him to stick his rod and balls out. In his hand was a wolf puppet. It was furry and orange-brown. Anything else didn't matter because my eyes were riveted to that pink human penis in a grey wolf puppet's mouth.

He was Korean. ID-ed by his extended appendage, and that I was in the Korean Ome channel. He wasn't small because it fitted nicely into that puppet's mouth. I guess he was Asian-average. I remembered thinking how it must feel. Maybe it was like rubbing your privates against soft wool or flannel.

He didn't say a word. I couldn't tell what head he had on since the screen showed his furry chest and waist down.

"I like your wolf." I grinned — way to break the ice by commenting on the obvious. I was hoping for a voice, but instead, he just jerked harder into that wolf's mouth.

I watched and posed. Unzipping my hoodie slowly and playing with my boobs. I enjoyed watching this furry masturbation. It wasn't every day I got to see this. I was hoping for an explosion.

Too bad. As always with Ome vid chat, before I got to see the best part, the screen switched.

And he wasn't the only weird one in a suit. Dog plushies surrounded a teenager on his bed. He was petting them and telling me about how much he liked them. And another was a popular Insta influencer who had a Judy Hopps fetish.

Yes, I remembered that bunny in the Zootop movie. I liked her from the start, and that flirting with that fox was Fire. I remembered asking H what those writers were insinuating. Yes, the sexual tension between the two animals was wild. I felt horny just watching them bicker and fight. Well, that was way before Yolo-ing and me knowing Furries were becoming a thing.

A long time ago, I went to Comic-Con and Anime-Con and watched the fans cosplaying their favorite characters. It was like Halloween except Asian style - anime, game characters, and Comic superheroes. All normal stuff. And sex that came with that, yes, it was sexy.

And then I started seeing Mascots, which I guess were what Furries were, starting to appear. The Japanese versions, with their anime and fantasy costumes, seemed hotter and more creative than the real animal suits. Never thought too much about them and didn't think it'd explode.

"Did you know Furry sex is becoming a thing?" A guy I met on a dating app once told me. He looked ordinary enough in person.

"Really?" At that time, I'd already heard more about that sexual genre. I'd read a thriller book, and there was a scene where the main character went to a Furcon. The book's descriptive words about the Yiff sex that went down were exciting, but I shrugged them off, thinking it was niche.

Initially, I thought Yiff was a word for another age fetish like Milfs, or Gilfs. And when I researched, I was surprised at the blooming genre with at least twenty million views for Yiff porn on the Internet.

This was a sexual movement.

I had to know more. Research, I called it. But, there was no unseeing those graphic real-life sex vids, some home-made vids of people in fursuits, 3d vids, and others cartoons. I had a thing for anime and manga. Claws were creeping up to drag me in.

After seeing those furry glory holes, it struck something deep in me, and I'm not into animalistic, hairy, and furry, but I got it.

Role play made sex fun. We were all animals. Dressing up as someone, something else, and going at it in full steam, rough, hot sex, be it in a suit or a maid costume, all wild, fantastic fun.

Why stop at just one suit? Why isn't everyone dressed in suits? Why not just gang-bang the shit out of it? Mass explosion of cum and juices, growling, roaring, and screaming — hairy, furry mess.

It could be cathartic.

We were oppressed by society and the faces we had to wear, so what was one more mask? The long and short is to be what you want to be.

In Ome, I saw Spiderman smoking and jerking off, and another person in a God suit. One wrapped in the flag of South Korea, and a few guys in maid costumes.

Yes, guy maid costumes were a thing. A few of the guys I'd chatted with had sprung that on me. Sending me pics of them in tight maid uniforms and their dicks poking like tents on their white aprons or splayed out on the ground. One had a skirt lifted with his oily stick in his hand.

"I thought it was just a meme. Guys in maid costumes," Someone said.

"No, dude. They are real. And they jerk off in them," I said. "And they like wearing those dresses for me." I bit my lip. It was hard to say how I felt.

Disappointment. Curiosity. Dirty.

Why? What attracted them to these outfits? Don't they want the girls to wear them? Why would they cross-dress? Why do some guys like wearing bras and panties?

These hot guys whom I'd imagined playing one day, and one I'd done, had that kink alternative. And, I'm open to whatever they liked, but the double standards in me weren't as open to having sex with them in those outfits.

Would it be better if they wore a fursuit instead?

"I'm very straight," I told some of the online guys. "I won't do a threesome with a girl. It's not my kink."

Which was true. We like what we like and who we like. I said several times before that I was a sex racist.

"I'd like to think I'm not racist, but sex is the one thing I feel I can be without feeling guilty about it."

They always laugh when I say that.

"I deserve the right to whom I should bang." But even as I proclaimed that, I tried to be fair. Experimenting with all things relatively equal, which I'd talk about in another story.

Was it troubling? People had types. Girls have types, but apparently, guys were freer for all. The world was a buffet, and having sex with a girl from every country was a colored pin on the global map.

"I am a fair and equal lover," H liked to say.

So, was I being fair to the Maid role-player guys? I don't know. Would it be better if they were dressed as animals with dicks sticking out? I don't know.

We had our preconceived notions about what we imagined people to be like. The bias that very hot guys were there to fulfill a woman's ultimate fantasies. It was unfair. Looks didn't guarantee a smooth, deliciously orgasmic night in bed. Experience had told me that.

Was I fulfilling my role as the hot, curvy Milf that everyone wanted?

Was loving Furries, wanting to be one, and fucking in a fursuit bad?

There was no right or wrong with sex. If anything, being Open was what made it fun and special. Memories were meant to be made and shared.

So, if it pleases you to wear that suit, do it. Be free, my friend.

For once, twice, or thrice, let those furballs hang.

—oo—

ONE CUP RANDY

—oo—

"We are Asians. Use a rice cup," I said.

"I'm thinking of spending my whole week cumming as much as I can. My roommate is leaving for Korea tomorrow," Cup said. "I'm going to be naked and hard all day. Going to try and have more orgasms than you."

"Omg. Streaking. I will be home alone, too. Shall we do a vid call together?" I asked.

"Maybe," Cup gave a smiley face. "Maybe I'll start cumming into a cup, and once I fill it up, you have to meet me."

Cheeky bugger. I'd been saying 'no' to him because he was a super sub.

"What type of cup?" I asked.

He was the third guy I met in my local quest to find a Fwb in my city. We chatted on Bumble, and he suddenly asked to meet. There wasn't time to dress sexy or plan what to say. In ten minutes, I was in my car, and in five minutes, I met him.

He checked some of the boxes. Korean. Yes. Young? 33 years old. Single? Divorced. We didn't talk much about it, but it didn't sound like a fun experience, and he was glad it was over.

When we met, we talked about everything except the one question I wanted to know — was he a pervert?

It was hard to tell. He was slightly taller than me, slim with glasses, dressed fashionably, not messily dressed in track pants, and with unwashed hair. Yes, I had those.

He bought me a hot chocolate, and we skimmed talking about sex till the end when we got into his car because he didn't want to leave until we had some personal time away from the others at the coffee shop.

"Can I touch your breast?" he asked daringly.

It was broad daylight, and his car faced the path most people took to the coffee shop.

"Okay...quick," I said. It was my second time having a guy touch my boobs in a car. The first was with the Cuck guy.

He gave a good squeeze, and my phone rang. I had to leave. It was time for school pickup.

When I got home, I was flooded with messages from him, and he told me he had an ex-Domme who bought him a Penis cage and locked him up. He'd been pegged and loved being tied up by her.

"I don't think we fit," I texted him. "I'm not a Domme like that. I love playing with young men, but I stop at pegging and definitely won't use a Penis cage..."

He kept sending me vids of himself jerking off to my vids and pics I'd shared. Using his Fleshlight to masturbate, knowing how I loved watching him cumming.

The Fleshlight was a rubber tube similar to Tenga's toys, and you could squeeze lube into it. His favorite was a clear tube with an open end. I loved watching him shoot from the other side.

"So you'll meet me if I fill a cup of cum?" he asked.

I couldn't stop laughing. It was so ridiculous. "Sure, but dude, you didn't say what cup."

He took pictures of all the different cups. Beer glass, soju shot glass, rice cup, and a tiny sake cup. I watched him as he played with the cups, trying to fit his cock in them.

"You're gonna lose," I laughed.

"I have lots of cum. I'll win," he boasted.

Sex shouldn't be taboo. Talking to a guy and being friends didn't have to be so difficult.

I was changing. One more foot out from the bubble of my daily suburban life. The cracks in the masks that I had to wear.

It wasn't just me. H and I were metamorphosing.

"You look different," many people have said. "You lost a lot of weight. You look happier now," they added. It felt awesome.

"What's happened with H?" His colleagues asked me.

"Why? He's happier," I replied.

"Is it a midlife crisis?" asked his secretary. They have been watching him from the windows of the office as he crossed the street below, wondering where he was going after lunch at work.

"Where is he going every day?" another asked.

I smirked. Probably to meet another new girl from a dating app, I wanted to say, but I didn't. This was our secret. No one knew of our double life then.

Back to the cups. "The rice cup. Use that." I chose the pic from the texts he sent me. "If you fill it up in a week, I'll meet you." I grinned.

"Alright. Deal," he said, giving a smiling emoticon back.

Bets. Dares. Challenges. My blood sang. This was who I was becoming. Cheeky, naughty, and damn right sexy. The jokes, roasting, and funny mean. Not needing to be sensitive. I loved it to the core.

"Bad news!" Cup messaged the day after our talk.

"Why? You couldn't do it?" I asked.

"No. I did. I cummed once in it yesterday. But…Urgh. Had to trash the cup," he said.

"Oh no…Didn't you put it in the fridge?"

"No…why?" he said.

"Oh.my.god. Where did you put it?" I asked.

"I hid it on my shelf behind my books," he said.

"But why? No one's home. Dude. Sperm is biological. If you don't fridge or freeze it, it'll rot."

"Oh…I didn't think of it. Isn't it gross to put that in your fridge?"

"You got to ziplock it."

"Yuck," he said. "It's body liquids…"

"Dude, how do you think moms keep breast milk? Or labs keep blood and whatever."

"Well…I eat from there," he said.

"If you can't handle that, you're not ready. Guess fate is not yours. We'll never meet."

Yeah. And so One Cup Randy was all talk — in less than a day, he was a cup out of luck.

TO PEG OR NOT TO PEG

He was an Executive at a very famous company.
I called him Aussie.

A name I gave him because he was the first white man I added to my IG. An Australian man I met on Ashley Madison (AM), a cheating site where married couples and singles looking for more mature men and women go to get laid.

There wasn't any subtlety to it. AM made Tinder look like a place where teenagers hung out. On AM, these adults were horny for a quickie and more kinks. To explain why I was on AM is a long story. Being new in the world of casual sex, I, baby cougar, had lots to learn.

Aussie.

Now, he was a veteran. He knew the cheating landscape well and coated his niceness with ease and friendship. Unlike many of the rude, horny white guys on AM, Aussie was a gentleman, and perhaps because he was a foreigner just as I was and wasn't so in-your-face about his Asian fetish because he liked all types of women, that smoothed the path. This smart guy got past my gate when I specifically said I'd only date East Asian men from 25-35.

Good old Aussie was neither East Asian nor young. At forty-eight, he was also older than I, which meant he failed to make the mark. But, he was charming, funny, and horny with his 'movies,' which were mostly him jacking off. Aussie had some hot videos of Asian women he banged to share.

It was a slow warm-up. First, he began by asking for my fit advice. Aussie said he'd taken some pics of himself and wanted a woman's opinion on which type of pic was attractive to other women, since I wasn't interested in him. That led up to his fetish for heels, and my story about a guy I spoke to who had a hot, Latin Fwb who only had sex with her stilettos on.

A few days of naughty tales and vid exchanges, and then the billion-dollar question came.

"Would you peg me?" he asked, so casually. Like, did you bring your umbrella? It's about to rain.

"It would be so hot if you peg me with heels. I'll buy you some." And as he was searching for the red heels to match whatever he thought I'd do for him.

"Peg?" I spoke out loud. I'm thinking the only peg I knew was the one you used for hanging clothes.

"Do you know what pegging is?" I asked a friend I was chatting with.

"What? Who said that?"

"Aussie is asking me to peg him," I said.

"Holy fuck. You sure he said that?"

"Yes, holy serious." I shook my head, and before I could say more, Aussie sent over a pic of black knee-high boots.

"This would look good on you. Wear the boots and that black corset."

"No." I messaged back. "I can't wear heels. Sorry. I'd fall..." By this time, I'd already googled the word, and my face was burning.

"Come on. This is my bucket list. My one wish."

"Dude. I just googled pegging. Are you crazy? I'm not gonna do it."

"With a strap on. I'd be on my fours."

And he sent a pic. A hot Asian Domme woman with a black patent leather strap-on and whip. A large white guy on his fours. A medium-sized dildo hanging from her pelvis. An abomination of nature, and I wouldn't care what people wore other than the image of me wearing it, which made me sick.

I had to close my eyes. "I'm not going to do that."

"You can." Aussie dropped a smiley and a naughty face. "I've decided. You are that hot and sexy woman who'd do it for me."

"And I decided. There is no way. Absolutely no way, I'm not wearing that fucking strap-on."

And so it began. Aussie's wooing. The quest to make me the baby koala he'd always wanted. That's what I called the action I'd take if push came to shove and he couldn't find another woman to take my place.

Baby Koala. I wasn't going to hump him from the top. A slide in might work if I could get past my uncertainty. I'm the baby, and the guy's the mommy. You get the point.

Months later.

"I found her!" Aussie was excited.

I grinned. Aussie's sexcapades were what kept us talking. His and his morning boners and the movies he'd always asked me to share. He was going on his Asian trip soon for work and was lining up his girls like joining the dots.

"A Japanese woman. She is a Domme, and she said she'd peg me."

"Whoa…really?" I was surprised that our friend was checking off his bucket list faster than I was.

"That's awesome, dude! So, how did you meet her?"

"Tinder. She said, "We'll go shopping for a toy together."" Though he was texting, I could hear his excitement.

"Is she gonna wear those heels? Damn. She's gonna deflower you."

"Yeah. Yeah…"

"I'm happy for you. Don't forget to take some pics."

"I'll make a movie for you."

Perverts unite. That's what we all were. We were from Ashley Madison, where I first met him. Those seeking to cheat and desperate for sex were the most perverse of them all. Perhaps age had to do with it. Or the pool of finding someone who was sexually active over thirty was harder than finding a bone in a haystack.

I was happy for him. Getting goals checked off before he'd hit fifty. I'd want to get all my bucket lists checked off by then, too. I'm not saying I was ready for all my fantasies, but it was good to know I'd have a new list to make after achieving my first.

Time passed.

"We had sex. We bought the toy…" Aussie texted.

"But you didn't do it?" I asked. "Bummer. Why?"

"Yeah. But I had five in a week," he boasted.

"That's a buffet, dude." I was expecting more. The movies he shared left much to be desired, but it was a feat for him to nail five women in three Asian countries. Again, it showed white dudes getting all the luck, while my tall, handsome, intelligent, artistic, Asian H was having a harder time nailing one.

To peg or not to peg?

Aussie wasn't the only one who wanted my help. He was the first, but wasn't the last. In the year since I started my journey, I've been approached more than ten times by different guys, of various ages and professions. To everyone's surprise, these men were straight. They were not closeted. They didn't like men. These were their reasons:

Top five reasons for pegging:

1. The feeling of dominance in a woman
2. Male orgasm
3. New sexual experience
4. Closeness of a lover
5. Playing with sexual toys

I believed that talking about sex opened doors to a person's innermost character and secrets they'd not share with anyone. I am privileged to be part of each one of their feelings, thoughts, and passions.

I did not judge. I did laugh. I embraced their words and shared my feelings and thoughts. If we were of the same vibe and mind, I was happy to play with them. Having chatted with hundreds, I knew what my preferences were. Saying no is always hard. No one likes rejection or giving it.

An angelic-faced Korean guy texted me after we matched. "I bought these two…" He sent me a picture of two dildos — a white one and a black one. Both were larger than the average Asian penis. One was half the girth of my fist.

"Have you used them?" I asked, surprised because it was the norm now to chat about the unexpected.

"I want you to use it on me." The twenty-something-year-old sent a smiley. "Noona, I want you to be my first."

First. Was it a perverted dream? A Milf initiation. Maybe I

should check out the Milf porn to better understand where this freakiness is coming from.

Submissives were more complicated than Doms. Yes. It was unfair. Do men feel they have to be in charge in the bedroom because society expects them to be? That being said, the subs had to feel comfortable telling me what they wanted because the women they met probably expected them to rule.

"You are the first person I've told about my sexual preference. No one, not my family or friends, knows how I feel. I worry that there is something wrong with me."

Many had said that. It felt good to be their confidante. There was nothing wrong. Sex was the one thing, the one secret key to the door of your inner self. I was and am grateful for the sharing and likewise shared what I could because I understood.

"When can we meet? I want you to peg me."

I blinked. "Isn't this fast?" I asked. I wasn't ready for this. If sex with a stranger was a step out of a normal relationship, then pegging went deep.

"Sorry, I can't," I said. "I'm not into pegging…and those dildos…don't they look too big?"

"You don't like me? Noona, why? I like you. Please do it when you come to Korea." The young Korean guy begged.

"No. It's not that," I replied. "I'm not a Femdom. Plus, I'm not attracted to doing this."

Rejection was hard, especially if the other person felt insecure.

Truth was, I was just as new as he was. Baby cougar had fields to run, and forests to tread. Heart soft and adventures to go, but pegging wasn't one of them.

─o THOUGHTS o─

My high was only reaching new heights — someone new, something different, a thrill I'd not had before.

I wanted everything. Greed was what I craved. My mind is open to all possibilities. No end in sight.

My eyes were different. The suburban bubble wasn't enough. Cracks in clear glass, the addiction was getting real.

I was happy. I was sensual. I was the cougar. Leaving bodies satiated as I sprinted through the mountains beyond, the air fresh and sun shining high above my new skin, my confidence fed.

The power was in my grasp. For once in my life, I felt alive. Not saying the journeys I'd untaken before weren't much, but each had a purpose and gave happiness in its own way.

This. This type of freedom. Unshackled and wholly me, myself, and the world.

For once, I wielded the power to move the bodies and minds of others. I gave happiness, shared sadness, and felt pain. Stories grew from my steps, flowers burst from my feet.

We were changing.

H and I were loving ourselves and each other more. Going on dates, having naughty fun, and opening our thoughts and feelings about all things. We were being selfish, treasuring our time and our alone journeys instead of giving them up for our family. Happiness spread like the rays of the sun. Our smiles were shared with our children and those around us.

Time was fast-forwarding. Full speed ahead through the first year as I bolted towards the new me, a race to Korea — Seoul, where I'd find the dreams I seek.

We were unconventional. We were empowered. And we weren't looking back.

CHAPTER FOUR

CHEATS AND FLICKS

CATFISH CURRY

"**A**re you a guy pretending to be a hot Korean guy with sex slaves?"

"I'm not!" he replied. "I'm Korean."

"That's what he said, too," I replied.

"I've a Korean name." I could feel his annoyance in his text. Sometimes I felt like trolling, and this was one of those days.

"I know of two guys, one white and the other brown, who had Korean names."

"You saw my profile and Instagram pictures," he said.

"I did, but I was just catfished, and I need more proof," I said. It wasn't fair that most guys got to see what I looked like, but they weren't willing to do the same. Yes, I understood their paranoia, but what about me?

"What is catfish?" he asked.

"Search it," I said.

"They don't treat you as real. See how they drop you like that. They don't care," advised a guy.

Dropping like flies. A mayfly lasts two days. I should be proud that I could keep my fish hooked for longer than that. Been three years, and some are still swimming in my tank. A feat, really. My racy content sustaining the feeding.

Being somewhat newb in the online world and two hundred percent more than naive, I was still falling for the "maybe I'd meet a new friend" mode.

Do unto others as you want others to do unto you.

Shit. If only people followed that rule. Maybe that's why good people are good suckers.

"I can be whoever I want to be online," said the catfish.

"Yeah. You can, but when truth comes to the shove, it's time to let up."

It all started with a red flag of my own making. There has to be a rule for this because I fell into the trap twice that day. Once was with a Korean cop, too hot to resist, and the other was this Korean dude.

Rule: Never randomly pick strangers on Instagram to make friends. Unless you knew more, it was hit-or-miss. More misses than hits, honestly.

At least, from the video chat channel or dating apps, the guys are bound by rules and ID verified. Though one could argue that filters and AI tech can completely change a person's looks, you might as well be talking to an avatar.

It is the human condition to connect with another real person. That's why idols exist, and I'm not discounting the realness of anime or game characters, plushies, or, for the kinks, their furries and sex dolls.

To each his/her/their/me/you, our own.

So in this case, he, the guy with a Korean name, is a hot Korean guy with sex slaves. Except he was not, far from it. Until now, I felt justified in lashing out at the man who lied through his teeth, and after blocking him and checking up on him, he was still faking under his same ID.

On the day I met him on Insta, he had over two hundred women of different races. He had fun travel pics in Europe. He loved biking, and his statuses were in Korean, and comments from those pretty women showed he was popular. Panoramic picture shots of him travelling and with shades on seem normal enough.

I followed him because I was surprised a hot guy like him was in my Insta recommended. We started chatting fast. My usual sex talk and the Byeontae game dropped like a bomb in close to ten minutes of DMing.

He read me like a book. The cougar barely shed her claws, and he was already on to me. He asked if I'd like BDSM, and I have yet to show him my naughty Insta. My normal pics alone usually wouldn't have triggered that ask. Nice, personable, mommy-looking me, or so I thought.

"Light bdsm. Spanking, rope, a little choking, cuffs," I replied. "U?"

"Yes, me too. My gf likes nipple clamps."

"Oh. Those hurt." I scowled. I tried them before those pesky metal suckers. They were nothing like the teasing bite of a sensuous mouth.

"The more painful, the more she liked," he said.

"Really?" In my head, I was imagining a Korean girl with a slim physique with metal clamps to her small breasts and pert nipples. I saw her crying out each time this hot guy punished her.

At that time, I didn't think too much about how I couldn't see his face in his Insta pictures. His body was enough for me to tell he packed a punch - tight lean abs, long body, broad shoulders. Plus, casually talking about sex and BDSM in the earlier days of my journey made me excited. I was a novice, eager to snatch a super-hot Korean guy.

"She also likes handcuffs," he added, "And she likes to watch me have sex with other girls."

"Whoa. She does?"

"So you've done threesomes before?" I asked, my voice breathless as I tried to stay calm.

Now, this was a topic I was interested in. Be it male-male-female or female-male-female, the idea of having another added to the fun. I didn't care for the female-male-female myself because a cougar didn't share, and I was sure I wasn't into girls. Still, all sex stories were always welcomed.

When the guys asked me to do threesomes with girls with them, this was what I said, "Ask me again if I like girls, and I'd ask you if you wanna be taken down by a guy during sex."

"I won't like it," they often said.

"It won't be pretty. I'd punch her face if she tries to hump me." This usually stopped the guys who were overly enthused about seeing their favorite Milf going at it with another girl.

"I like finding the girls and making them my slaves," Catfish guy continued.

"You hunt them," I grinned to myself. I could relate to this: the thrill of finding and securing someone new.

He liked them curvy. My ego was brushed with his smooth talk.

Objectification.

I had absolutely no issues with that.

It's part of the sexual attraction. The media and fashion peeps were mistaken to think only scrawny-assed women and buffed guys were all that. Power to those who learned that beauty came in all forms and sizes and loved in all their ways and positions.

I wished I had known this earlier — that curvy was always in. Big boobs and ass are always sexy. And whatever my Asian mom and relatives berated me for when growing up, I wasn't fat.

In a warped way, the Asian elders thought that was a good learning experience. There was always room for improvement. If we could take the verbal and psychological bullying from the people closest to us, we could take on anything and, one day, as they planned, rule the world.

Too much ego was weak. Humility with thought was a double-edged sword.

"To win one hundred victories in one hundred battles is not the acme of skill. To subdue the enemy without fighting is the acme of skill." — Sun Tzu.

Thinking back, Catfish guy wasn't the super dom he thought he was. In fact, he was ruled by his Domme — the nipple clampee. If he were smart enough, he'd know women are manipulators, and she was the one pulling his balls.

"The quiet ones are the best," Catfish guy said proudly. "They look at you shyly and are the last to leave. They are the most perverted."

"How do you meet these shy types?" I asked.

"Friends of friends and other social gatherings," he said.

"And how do you ask her to join ur 3some fun?" I asked.

"It takes time and patience. I'm never in a hurry," he replied.

"Ah…you like to play with your prey."

"Yes. I make her want me. Get her wet. She has to tell me she wants to have sex with me first."

"And how do you find one more girl? Do you pick two of your slaves and then do it?'

"No, no. They are usually friends."

"Friends? Isn't it harder?"

"Friends like each other, so the next step to having sex together is easier."

"Interesting." I wondered if it worked with men, too. I didn't want gay action. Just like I'm not into women, I don't expect my boys to like each other sexually. In fact, in the game of sex, Power Play was one of the highlights.

"You're not sexually positive. You, of all people, should be open to all types of sex," said someone.

"I choose what gets me off. I wanna hear their stories, but I don't have to be part of it."

Catfish and I spent two more days chatting. I showed him my naughty Insta and told him more stories about the people I'd met. Sharing sex vids and talking about what type of sex I liked. He flirted with me a lot, and eventually, we were sexting. It was obvious he was trying to reel me in.

My ego said I shouldn't. It'd be playing into his hand, but I was curious and didn't want to wait any longer. "Let's meet."

The next morning, I wore my lingerie under my blue hoodie when we met online. We talked about plans to finish off where we stopped in our sexting.

I was nervous. Thinking he was a hot Korean guy I'd snagged. At our scheduled time, I called him on Insta. It rang a few times, and then he hung up my call.

"Hey," I said. "Why did you hang up?"

"My room is a mess," he said.

"So?" I replied. I'm not a neat freak, but I don't like slops. I'd expect a guy I'm going to meet would take a little time to make himself presentable because I'd do the same. We knew we were planning to meet the day before. Planning was part of the chase.

"Aren't we gonna play?" I DMed.

"Yes. Yes," he replied.

I waited. Surfing the net and waiting ten more minutes.

"So? Are we?" Each minute that passed was a strike against him. My time was very precious. And lessons learnt too many times, I was a hungry cat, but I was worth the wait, and not vice versa.

Finally, he called. I watched the window to his room appear. It seemed normal enough, except it was missing the most important element.

"Hey! Where are you?" I peered into the screen to get a better look. "Aren't you too old to be playing hide and seek?" I laughed uneasily.

"Whoa..." he typed. "You are real."

I rolled my eyes. "Of course I am."

"You...you are so beautiful."

"Why? You get catfish a lot?" I smiled. "So..." I waved. "Come out and show yourself and stop typing."

At this point, even though I was being friendly, my heart was beating fast. The red bells were ringing in my head, and I'd lost my interest in playing.

"Hello." He finally spoke.

My heart dropped to the pits. Dark, dirty, and dungeony. "Holy fuck." That was what I thought, but years of training to treat everyone equally held the reins.

"K?" I spoke again, this time all fun and laughter gone from my voice.

"Yeah," he replied nervously. He still hasn't shown himself, but I already knew.

He was not a Hot Korean guy who had sex slaves; in fact, he wasn't even East Asian.

Now, don't get me wrong. I treat all people equally and have friends of many races. Girls or guys, whatever, it doesn't matter.

But, as I'd told many guys whom I chatted with, and I'd go into more details in my later chapters, I'm a sex racist.

Yes. Sex racist.

I don't sleep with guys other than East Asian. Well, at least at that point, when I'd met K, I hadn't found that one special guy to break the spell.

So, No. He wasn't East Asian. More like South Asian, as in from India. And like bees to honey, those guys in that region totally love me. I'm not joking. I'm being serious. Since I was young, it has always been the case, and till now, on dating apps, I get thousands of likes, and many South Asians are trying to get my attention. Thirsty, thirsty men.

"Wow. I really like you," he said.

My heart shriveled. I wanted to run. I wanted to yell at him for lying and for being an assholic cheat.

"Can you guess where I'm from?" he asked.

Dude, wasn't it obvious? In my mind, I'm praying with the slightest chance that he's a Korean who grew up in India and had that accent. But, of course, who was I kidding?

"India, dude," I said, my voice already sounding annoyed. "Why did you lie? And just show your face now. I'm showing mine in good faith."

"I'm not lying. I'm role-playing."

What-the-fuck?

And I'm too fucking nice to not slam down the laptop and, of all things, my conscience picked the moment to tell me I shouldn't reject so awfully because that would make me a racist.

I'm a nice girl. Super nice. Naive to the world of the Internet. Prancing around happily, flirting with guys, flashing my boobs, and more to give them a rise. I liked doing that. Be that sexy, naughty Milf. Blue-balling boys as I like.

But not that day. I had to be that Puritan, politically correct woman.

I won't bother you with the details. So, I let that jerk explain his way out of his ass on why pretending and lying to all the girls that he was Korean, and in another life, he wished he was Korean, was okay.

Now the pieces were fitting why he didn't want me to chat with that Korean cop.

"The Internet is a dangerous place. He might not be a real policeman, or maybe he is. He can track you down," Catfish K said.

Reverse image tracking. Now, that caught my attention more. But chatting with the Korean cop guy was too hard to resist. Kdrama and those Korean men stretching their uniforms with their jacked shoulders and chocolate abs.

This was a whole lot of Bull. As Catfish K was reciting his slave plans again, I got more disgusted with myself for falling for his stupid stories and lies.

"Okay, this is enough," I said, checking my clock. I gave him ten minutes. That should be enough to say I'm not a racist. "We are done."

"What? No. Please. You're so beautiful. I want to be your friend. I want to play with you." His voice dropped to a whine.

"You gotta be kidding me, right?" I glared at the empty room. "You won't even show yourself."

"Okay, okay! I will!" He sounded desperate now. And just as he was, or maybe was going to do it, I slammed my laptop down and blocked him.

Who cared if he showed his real face? In fact, seeing his face would make the memories worse. And he tried many times to follow me again, changing his Insta and whatnot. This cat-and-mouse game was getting annoying.

I kept my accounts private. Not only was I protecting myself, but I was also protecting the people who followed me.

Just the other day, he sent another message. It had been more than a year, and he wanted back into my naughty account. He asked if I remembered him.

Of course I do, Catfish K. You're the Indian guy who pretends to be a hot Korean guy with sex slaves — the loser we will all remember.

—oo—

HELMET

—oo—

I t was a cliche but with a twist.

This story wasn't mine, but it might as well be. A young man with a thirst for Milfs and a Milf-next-door who couldn't help herself.

I met him on Tinder, and he was twenty-four, living on his own in his parents' place. He'd graduated from the US and finished up more school before enlisting in the Korean army when we chatted. As always, the chats turned hot and heavy, and he confessed he'd been eyeing a Milf in his apartment.

"I think she likes me," he said.

"Why?" I asked.

"She's been wearing short dresses lately and smiling at me," he said.

"She likes being looked at," I replied.

"She's hot for sure. Damn. She has nice legs. Not as curvy as you, but she's hot."

Guys this age can be dumb when in heat. This one was no different, and I was a little surprised to learn he was a pro chess guy. However, it made sense because if you grew up dedicating yourself to one sport, be it physical or mental, socially, you'd probably not be as wise.

"So what's the plan?" I asked.

"I'm going to talk to her," he said.

God, this guy. So cute when horny. But what do I know? I'd not approached a stranger in real life without dating apps.

Days went by, and I asked again. "So did you?"

"She kissed me!" He was so excited.

"Whoa. Where?"

"In the elevator! We were alone, and I talked to her, and she kissed me!"

"Is she Open too?" I had to know. From what I got, Open relationships were rare. However, my population of surveys could be skewed.

"No. It's a secret." Damn, this woman was steps ahead of me. Married and cheating. Didn't they say - don't poop where you sleep?

"So which floor does she live on?" I asked.

"Next door. We share the same wall."

"No f-king way." She won. It took guts. If I weren't Open, I wouldn't risk this. "Does she have kids?"

"No."

That explained everything. Women needed sex, too. And when there is a choice piece of young meat next door, why not, right?

The thrill of the chase. Corrupting the young, horny guy, was the best way to get over life's unhappiness and screw the husband who probably contributed to 50% of that said bad life.

Women these days work. If she were home with no kids, that meant a few things.

"So what's next?" I asked.

"We're going to meet a week from today. In the morning, when her husband goes on a business trip."

"Whoa. Sounds like a plan."

I was excited for him. This was drama coming into true life. I was popping the popcorn and pulling a chair to sit. I had to witness this. The front virtual seat was as close as I could get.

"What are you gonna wear?" I asked.

"Should I shave?" He asked.

Hilarious. "Does she like shaved?" No. We are not talking about a beard. So cute that he is concerned if she liked him clean as a babe down below or hairy like a man.

"I don't know…what if I cum too fast? The last time I had sex was a year ago. What if I can't satisfy her? She's so hot. I jerked off last night thinking of her."

The dude is so into lust. I could see her having him wrapped around her finger. I giggled thinking of him getting so excited and cumming fast like an adolescent puppy.

Was that why I liked them young?

Lately, I'd been thinking I had had enough of the very young. Experience had its benefits. But the most important was the ability to edge and knowing how to either cum many times quickly or hold enough for me to have my fun. And not many, even the older ones, knew how to satisfy a woman or cared enough to.

The Queen can only be benevolent for so long. Weighing the need to corrupt vs. the need to be satisfied. A tough choice to make.

Back to Chessboy.

"OMFG!" Came to the text in a few days.

"What? What's happened?" I asked.

"Her husband read our dirty chats! He knows."

I could have said — I told you so. My gut told me that this guy was reckless and in their haste to the finish line, and sensing why this Rapunzel was stuck in her condo castle, the husband was no joke. He was the mobster you didn't want to mess with.

"So, now what?" I asked.

"I've been hiding in my apartment. I've not gone out in four days!"

"Are you serious? What about school?" I asked.

"I can take most of the classes online. I told my professors I'm sick."

"Dude, you have to leave at some point."

"I called delivery. I'm running out of toilet paper. I tried hearing when he left. What if I see him in the elevator?"

"He probably has 9-5 hours, right?" I asked.

"No. He sells medical supplies. His hours are not fixed."

This was getting ridiculous. "Dude, you picked a guy who could come home anytime and catch you in the act?"

"She was coming to my place. She'd pretend to go out and come home after, but the walls are thin."

Of course, they were. Cheaters would be caught at some point. Karma was a bitch.

"What am I gonna do? I'm so stressed out! I can't study. I'm failing my classes. My parents will know if he tells them what I did."

"Did? You haven't done it yet." I pointed out.

"But those texts. They are sex texts. We sent pics and vids. She's been contacting me. She still wants to fuck."

Well, all I could think was that the woman was as much to blame and seemed like she was still alive to be this cruel.

I didn't like her. Selfish, horny, stupid bitch.

"I still want to have sex with her," he said.

"Ofc you do. She is hot, and you're thinking with your cock, Dude. She isn't the only Milf. You are in so much trouble.

It's not worth wasting your life for one woman who is already taken with an unstable husband. Or she might be unstable too, you know."

"You have a point...so now what?"

"Go apologize. Get on your knees. You Koreans do that right?" Yeah, thank Kdrama for that.

"Tell him it was a mistake and that you'd never go through with it and won't see or touch her ever."

"But what if I still want to?" he asked.

"Can you move?" I asked him.

"No. This is my parents' place."

"Exactly. Don't embarrass your parents." Was he for real? This was the point when the loser was written on his head. I should drop him, but the drama was too good to miss.

The next few days of silence, and then a DM popped up.

"He wants to meet."

"So, when? Where?" I asked.

"Tomorrow morning. Outside his door."

"Good. Grow up and do what you gotta do."

"Okay...maybe I should wear a helmet."

"Helmet?" That left me in hysterics. "Helmet?"

"Yes. So if he hits me, my brain won't be smashed."

"Good point. A pro chess player shouldn't lose his head. Wish you thought of that instead of your cock."

"Not funny." He hated to be teased.

"But it is! So funny!"

And then there was silence. I shouldn't have pushed his buttons too much, and I missed the climax because of that.

Now I do not know what happened, and just when I thought

it was the end, he appeared on Bumble a year later, and we connected again.

"Pro chess guy!" I said the moment our chats started.

"You remembered."

"Of course! No, every guy wears a helmet and confronts an angry husband."

"Hahaha."

"So what happened?"

"Nothing much."

And that was how it went. He was not willing to confide and instead asked for my pics and vids, and I wouldn't give them if he didn't reveal the secrets I wanted.

Yes, what a downer. Not exactly the reason why you read this story to begin with, so being a giving Milf, I'd end you with this.

Let's call it a Fantasy moment.

Close your eyes and imagine this.

I was the hot and dirty Queen instead of that spoiled, unstable Rapunzel in that Aparto castle.

Start with our meeting in the elevator. I was wearing a dress — black and summery with lace and a square cut front so you could see my big, blooming boobs. A dress length above my knees and raised higher on the back because my wide ass needed more cloth to cover its delectable curves.

"Chessboy, right?" I'd say because I'm the cougar and I can't wait for shy, lusty boys to make the first move.

"Erm…yes." He looked at me with his glasses and then away. The elevator door closed, and from the first to the twenty-second floor, there was enough time.

I shifted to his side to pretend to check the buttons. He stepped back, and I turned to him as I brushed my hand through my hair. The scent of my shampoo and perfume filled the gap between us.

"I know you're watching me." I dropped my hand and touched his. Our eyes are not leaving each other. Our fingers curled together, and he grabbed my hand with one, and the other wrapped around my waist.

Tingles everywhere as I looked up, and then stared at his lips, opening mine slowly to breathe. He dropped his head, and our lips touched. Both were hungry as we ate each other like beggars needing air.

My hands were treading his hair as I tiptoed to get more of him, pressing my body against his hard chest and legs, and pushing my breasts against him when he released my lips and attacked my breasts. I tilted my head back, he held my waist with both hands, and one hand dropped to grab my ass as my nipples popped from my dress (I didn't wear a bra) and took one rose-colored nipple at a time with his lips, sucking hard on my sexy pebbles as I moaned.

Eighteen, nineteen, I stepped back, took his hand, and brought him under my skirt. Fingers smoothly up my thick, silky thighs and then to the wetness of my folds. (No panties)

Lights flashing. Twenty, twenty-one, twenty-two.

The elevator door cranked open.

"See you," I said with my sexy, breathless voice and stepped out.

—oo—

DICK PARADE

—oo—

It was a dick parade.

Each guy was flaunting unasked-for pics — different shapes, sizes, lengths, colors, and hairiness. Cheating app Ash was filled with these uncalled-for shots.

The Year 2023 was definitely my first parade, and life would never be the same.

Ash was my first dating app, and my first foray. Hundreds of requests from the thirsty cheating husbands and boyfriends desperately looking for some action. In those texts were some not-so-nice words because Ash was silently pimping us women into commodities in their attempt to bring in more male users. Women sign up for free, and guys pay to text a woman to chat with her on the app.

I was curious because in the sea of cheaters, there were young single guys with kinky desires who loved Milfs.

From the years on after 2023, one thing became clear: there was a pattern/culture of men in the apps. I know this might sound prejudiced, but from my experience, white men had the ego and dropped unasked-for dick pics; the blacks were cool and loved showing their sex vids; the latinos talked a lot about their families and were sweet and fast horny; Indians were pushy, boastful of their creds and super thirsty; and East Asians were shy, curious, closetted pervs and worried about size Queens, and short Kings.

My first dating app and observation of a herald of horny guys in Ash was white culture. I'm not gonna splice this nicely or be politically correct. White men loved to show their dicks. And white men also loved Asian women, and with the combo of Asian woman, Milf, big boobs and ass, and cougar, I was massive lint.

Everywhere online dating, women had the upper hand with their hand-picking of hot to decently above average guys. As many guys complained, it was fucking unfair that even the average, mediocre woman who wouldn't get even a second glance on the street could play princess online. Men were desperate because competition was stiff, and it also didn't help that the Ash app was filled with bots and scammers.

So, for the first three months on Ash, I answered my fan messages. Roasting some slowly, and others heading straight to the chopping block.

I uploaded pics of myself in my lingerie. The crowds went wild whenever I dropped a photograph in my AM profile. I was kicked off the platform four times and banned. I petitioned, looked for loopholes, got back in, and was kicked out again. Some loser probably whined about me not giving him his money's worth of messages.

I was for the Team Young-East-Asian boys. And here were some of my greatest roasted hits:

Name: Heavyasseater
Age: 26

My message to him:
At first, I read it as HeavyAsset, which is okay, I guess, for an ID, till those crossed eyes righted themselves, and bam! U like to eat asses!

Interesting. Different from the average Joe. So what kind of ass do u like to eat? Bigger the better, or tight little puckers, so I'd be kissing those red lips down below? Haha. I'm caught, but I'm serious. I'm assuming that's ur kink because it isn't every day that u meet an ass-eater. And when did u learn u have this fetish? I'm not judging. Just curious. My fetish is a little out there too, maybe not as urs, but still in the wildness looking for a home. Sounds to me like we could be pals. XD

Message 2:
I know I should wait, but the questions keep coming. Is that profile pic real? This site is flooded with bots. I can't even be sure this profile is urs. Maybe some user retention person is pulling ideas out of his/her butt and decided to post this profile to gain more traffic. Okay, those two private pics and that I'd admit proud cock don't match ur look. Stock pics? Photoshop? What's going on? Curiosity eats this pussy.

———

Name: MDbigD
Age: 34

Profile:
"MD with a big D, hoping not to run into any of my patients here!" Athletic, looking for some

discreet fun. Good with my hands and know my way around a body, can thank medical training for that.

My message to him: I've been thinking. This pic has to be a bot. But then, when I read ur profile, it's too funny not to be real. Yes, hands are great. I love them when they are on me, in me, and knowing where to touch. Don't want them too close to my heart, tho. And I'm talking literally.

—

Name: NotYourTypicalGuy
Age: 24

Profile: "Your outfit would look great on my bedroom floor."

My message to him: Love it. U know what else will be great on the floor? My knees. :D Or maybe urs? I'm guessing you're real. The last ten msgs I sent to those Asian boys with my sharp wit haven't responded. It'd be a waste if it were those bots who saw them. :) So, how much of a pervert r u? We should compare fetishes. Seems like that's a sure-fire way to get to the point. I'm not into polite words n mushiness. I save that talk for my husband, which, btw, I'm a Milf or a cougar looking at ur age. And don't ask me how old I am. I'm sick of lying. :D Anyways, I'm always up for some wild fun n spanking is only the beginning.

Message 2:
Now, having been suspended once by AM for goodness knows what reason, I'm beginning to suspect the sly things they do. Why are you in my sent messages when this is my first time sending you a message? Okay, I lied. I sent you one earlier this morning, but then, flash, I lost my account. I was barred from AM like I'm the dirtiest slut in the world or some hooker when I'm just an ordinary, horny Byeontae housewife who is spending her Sundays mass messaging guys on AM. :D Anyways, my new profile is loading, and sorry for the long message. I'm trying to save you credits. See? I'm nice. Message me if you want to know more about what we can do together. Sex doesn't have to be complicated. Just funny and super mind-blowing hot.

Message 3:
I wished I could say those profiles on Ashley Madison (AM) were all real. In the world of AI and bots, we would never know. Until I met them, these guys could be just ones and zeros, created from the words of desperate employees of AM.

—

Name: MakeItInteresting
Age: 37

My message to him: U definitely made it interesting with that shiny d pic. But more than that, does she know u r using that pic to hit up more girls on here? I'm not judging. We're in purgatory together, living in sin, raising the roof. Actually, maybe I'm not because hubby here said I should reply to ur msg bec that's one amazing...d...profile id. XD Alright, I'm just dropping a line. Not into hooking up. Just prancing around showing my boobs because, as someone said, I'm quite the exhibitionist.

Comment:
Now this guy answered. We had a convo, and he wanted to meet. But, just for the dick? His attitude had much to desire, so I said, No.

—

Name: kfever30
Age: 29

Profile: If you have yellow fever, but are looking for an Asian that doesn't fit the typical physical stereotypes, then I'm your man.

My message to him: You got me there. Yes, kfever isn't a joke. Been fucking a few online from ur motherland. :D If u r looking for a Milf, married and byeontae, then maybe we can hook up. I'm cute and super hot (according to the guys online), curvy with cup Ds, small waist, and big ass for doggying. My fav btw, harder the better. I'm very wild, so be warned in a happy, Open r/s. Knowing we r all Asians, closeted as always. So, I have to be discreet.

—

Name: Ribbit80
Age: 42

Profile: I love: ramen shops, boba, Netflix binging, 6 am HIIT classes, mocha donuts, lo-fi, hermit, anime, spam in fried rice, sake, and double expressos.

My message to him: I love: tall, hot East-Asian, crazy sex, laughing, all asian foods, otakus, dramas, and maybe you. Cheesy, yes. Rub it on me? Sure. Just not melted. :D So, I've been thinking, you must be a bot. In fact, all the Asian guys are bots. Honey pots to lure the unsuspecting Asian girls so those white men on AM can get their fetish dreams come true. Not forgetting the dirty grandpa pervs sending their scary dick pics.

Whatever excites me? Cucumbers excite me. Bananas, I love and big toes, well…let's leave it there. I'm a Milf. Open relationship, happily off on new adventures. I go for kinky sex, rough and dirty. If you like grabbing, my boobs and ass are doggy fun. And what's your favorite hentai? Mine's ninjas and assassins, and as for tentacles, not really, but I definitely get it. :D

Comment:
This guy was real and quite a character. He was divorced, rude, and full of himself. No doubt he was hot, and he knew it. He was single, seemed ready to move on, and expected me to meet his needs. The cougar didn't need a pampered prince, so he was dropped.

Ash ended as it came. Hot and sticky. I was ready for more, for more green pastures and miles ahead. I was on to the big dating apps.

SLAUGHTERED LIKE A PIG

I was once asked what my red flags were. After thinking about it, I said, "I'm a moth to the flame."

The red flags were everywhere, and yet, like the rabbit in Alice, I rushed to the finish line, knowing full well my head might be chopped.

I loved playing sexy games, juggling my wits when I shouldn't because a nice girl like me couldn't possibly defeat a nefarious Chinese organization.

Scammer hunters.

Maybe I'd been listening to too much rap music. Bravado lay in the balls I didn't have, and boredom was the bed I hid in to write this book.

So, where do I start? This tale of the big bad wolf? Maybe I should call it — 杀猪盘 — butchering the pig. This was a Chinese scam that would lead to fattening the pig (the victim) and then bleeding them dry with fake investments and crypto.

I had to know the scammers' dating playbook. I have been almost tricked once. You'd think once bitten, twice shy, but by the third, this was a hunting game.

Let's start with the first guy. His name was Dylan. Handsome like a Chinese drama actor. Most likely in his mid twenties, though he listed himself as early thirties, as they all did. To catch a lonely older "sister" to romance was in his KIP.

He was six feet tall, with sun-kissed, smooth Asian skin and an athletic build. Muscled, nicely toned, not bulky, with a V-shaped body and impressive dick.

Of course, his name meant nothing in retrospect, because he went by a few names after he booted me off. I reported him as a scammer and got him banned. Still, he returned, and his name was Dylan and then, Liam, and more, with the same profile, except his face changed like a chameleon. Profile the same, and then it was him again with the same face but a different age, profile, and location.

Having been a superuser on the dating apps for two-and-a-half years, I knew at a glance. There was a pattern to fishing, and I could go on about his playbook to catch his prey, but we all know what you want. So, let's get down and dirty.

Dylan and I began chatting as friends. He told me how lonely he was moving to Malaysia to study, leaving his home in Sichuan province. He talked about how tough it was growing up in a foreign country because he had to learn Malay instead of Chinese, and then I showed him my naughty Insta, and everything sped up in a flash.

"I think you're gonna be my favorite," he said.

"Wooo, I'm getting top place? Now we r becoming serious."

"Yeah," he replied.

"I'm seeing the 色狼 pervert man. Love it." I said.

"Do you want to come over here and have a nice night?" he asked. "Beauty. I'm very shy. I can accept your call, but I'm really shy about video calls. I dare not say those words face to face on video."

That's when I should have known. Already, the words he'd used in Insta were different from the dating app. As a writer, I was sensitive to nuances in dialogue and personality traits. Warning bells were ringing, and when we called again, I heard the sounds of metal.

"Is that a fan?" I asked. Winter was around the corner; there wasn't the need for more artificial wind.

"No. I'm outside alone. The moon is in the sky." I let him continue. His spoken Chinese sounded like a Beijing accent, thought he was from Szechuan and had lived in South East Asia for so long. Again, something wasn't right.

"We can do it in the darkest part of the night," he said. We talked about the best places to have sex.

"Not in my house," I said.

"Keep your groans down," he said. "I'll climb up the window and hide if your husband comes."

"Lol. I cannot keep my moans down. U can cover my mouth, but the sound comes out. Each time u push me, I will moan. Like a dog squeaker doll. U can duct tape my mouth n the sound still comes out."

"I wanna see your ass," he said. "I'm gonna pick you up and French kiss you so you don't make a sound. Babe, you are so sexy and beautiful. I'm already thirsty."

"Do you like squirting?" I asked, ego made me say it. The bells were ringing, but I was pulled by his leash. The pics he sent in between our convos and mine to him, adding to his reactions, was leading me on.

"I'm gonna fill this room with your dirty water. I want you to spray it all on my stomach, and then you and I shower together. Lmaooo…." he said. "I'll eat them all. Lmaooo…"

"Stomach is good. Leg is good too. I'll rub my wet pussy up

and down ur leg and suck ur cock and balls. I rain squirt. U'll need lots of towels."

"拍个视频 给我宝贝. 我的鸡巴又硬了. 这是你现在的吗 宝贝. 我要看你现在的样子." (Make a video, baby. My cock is hard again. Is this yours now, baby? I want to see what you look like now.)

His Chinese was coming out. In our call earlier, he said he spoke Chinese to people he was close to. Frankly, it didn't matter because my online translator was my best friend. Besides, it was fun watching sex told in Chinese.

"I'm a mess now. N H is sitting right in front of me." I lied because I knew it got most guys, and it got him, too. These young men like to cuck the husband or boyfriend. The thrills with the frills.

"It doesn't matter. That's how I like it. As long as it's you, I like it," he said.

"I'm hiding in the bathroom," I said.

"Let me see your pussy. 美女. 我很害羞 如果打电话我还能接受. 视频电话 我真的很害羞. 我单身太久了." (Beautiful girl. I am very shy. I can accept it if I call you. Video call. I am really shy. I have been single for too long.)

A red flag.

Romance scams. The play of tag. I kept asking to meet him in person. Video chat and then meet to do the deed. We discussed days and times on his calendar vs mine and his place vs. a hotel. At the back of my mind, I knew with this back and forth, and he was never going to meet me in person. The pushback was to keep me on for his final agenda.

"Are you sure it's not a scam?" H asked.

"Maybe," I said.

"Drop him," said H.

"Give me a day. I won't tell him anything," I said. Was it worth making H mad? No fish was that precious. But my curiosity and lust were getting in the way.

Which came first? The hunter or the fish?

Before our initial call, Dylan freaked out first. "Are you playing with my emotions?" he asked. "If I have sex with you, are you going to make me pay?"

"What?" I was shocked.

"You're tricking me, right?" he said.

I laughed. Wtf. "Are you for real? hahahaha! You think I'm a scammer?"

The irony of a scammer thinking I was hunting him. Which was true, and he was right to be afraid because the cougar didn't let go. A prey was most fun when there was the thrill of sex — the scent of hormones rising through the electronic waves and the longing for consummation within reach.

"Where do u live?" I asked. If he were on Bumble, I could have tracked his location, but I met him elsewhere. Even with his verification, it didn't mean he wasn't a fake.

"Didn't I tell you? 我住在你心里." (I live in your heart)

Another red flag. It was so cheesy that even a kid could spot it from a mile.

"My lips will not leave your body, will kiss along your thigh, lick your inner thigh. I like that you can cooperate with me to separate your legs gently, let me lick down, and kiss your calves. Kiss again! Inner thigh !"

This was scripted. The speech pattern changed frequently — another red flag. We were more casual-speak on the app. The

American slang was there, but not the Malaysian, which he should be using, partially because he'd been living there for more than a decade.

Sexting. Trading nudes and sex tapes. We did all those. He left his voice messages. Checked.

Was I desperate? I'd like to think I wasn't. This was the lure. Who was baiting whom more? I, wanting to catch this big fish, scammer or not, and thinking despite odds, I could reel him or them in.

Curiosity killed the pussy. Ego brainwashed mind. And after days of chatting and vid play, the day came as it should.

A different guy.

"Oh oh. Hope you are healthy."

"I am. I tested," I said. "Wanna meet?"

"I won't have sex with you if you are not healthy," he said.

"I'm all clean and healthy. I have test results. That's why I'm picky and why I like playing online. My guys are mostly in Korea."

"Oh oh. Do you want to play with me, Babe?" Duh. We have been talking about D-day for the last three days.

"Yes, but I don't just want to play. I want a Fwb. Good friends to hang out with and eat a meal. Not a one-night stand."

"Do you want me? Do you want me to be your boyfriend? Of course you can."

"It won't be fair to u," I said.

"Why is it unfair? You can stay with me while I work. I could take you along for the money."

"What? Money?" I was shocked at his confidence. His shame-lessness, despite knowing it was coming to this.

"Don't you see what I'm saying? I mean, I can talk to you when you are bored. I could take you along for the money."

"Is that a translation thing?" I asked.

"Because I'm doing some investment in my spare time, and I could take you with me. So we can have sex, and I can make money with you," he said.

Two things I never want to hear. I'm not always savvy, but this was something even a baby cougar knew.

Money. Investment.

Two words that should never be together in the same sentence.

"Hmmm…I think we need to speak in Chinese. This sounds different in English."

Would he do it? Translate?

Before, I was teasing and playing with a might-be crook. There was a minute chance he might not be who I always knew he was, but now, I was messing with a criminal or criminals.

He paused.

"Well, I can't travel with you. I can only hang out with u when u work at home. Or if we meet somewhere in a hotel between our homes," I said.

"我的意思是我会在我业余的时间里面做一些投资 当你和我在一起的时候 我们能享受到性爱的乐趣 我还能带你赚钱." (What I mean is that I will make some investments in my spare time. When you and I are together, we can enjoy sex, and I can also make you money.)

"你不明白吗?" (Do you understand?) He added when I didn't reply.

"Half-half. Why are you helping me make money?" I asked. He didn't get that I was playing a game. I saw how far he'd go before he realized his ruse was over, that I wasn't the pig he'd hoped to slaughter.

"I like you. Because you are good to me, I will be good to you. It's nice to chat with you, which makes me satisfied."

"I don't need your help to make money, Dylan," I said.

"Oh oh. You turned me down again. You r going too far?" he said.

He was talking about the time when he accused me of being a prostitute, and I said that if he thought I was selling myself, then we could just forget about it. Frankly, he's the one who didn't get it. I was in high demand. I didn't need him. I had many hot guys to play with, and the only reason why I was keeping on him was that the hunt was fun and catching a scammer was a thrill I didn't get every day.

It was time to end it.

"So what do you want to talk about? Just talk about sex?" The Scammer asked.

"No, but I'm not investing money," I said.

"Oh oh. Didn't you say you took my picture yesterday? Where are the pictures, babe?"

Huh? What the hell is he talking about? That "Oh oh" was annoying. More annoying was this new guy with his attempts to rectify fucking up.

"I want you now. I am very hard. Your pictures make me miss you. Babe."

"Dylan. Why r u not matched with me on the app anymore? I lost our chat history." This was the end.

"Make a phone call...wait!" he said, and he tried to call me, but I didn't pick up.

"Goodbye," I said and blocked him.

This pig escaped the cleaver by an inch, but the Scammer was faster. He had me reported, and I was blocked in my favorite app.

And did I learn my lesson?

No.

Moth to a flame. Moth to a flame. I loved red flags. Let the games begin.

ADULTRESS VIRGIN

"So who are you gonna choose? 24 or 34?"

It was a tough decision. Both had their pros and cons. It wasn't that long ago that I'd started the quest.

The journey to Yolo-ing. It was a decision both H and I made. And it was April 2023, and I was chickening out. Playing online and masturbating weren't the same as actually meeting a living, breathing person.

Ever since our one week of opening up in December and talking about everything under the sun — the good, the bad, and the fuckable, it was time to venture out.

H had been supportive of my morning vid chats with Korea and the guys I met online. Ometv reaped a bounty of fish, and I was thoroughly occupied for two days a week, and including the fun H and I were having, I was satiated and happy.

But it wasn't fair.

"The world is fucking unfair to Asian guys here. We are at the bottom of the totem pole," many guys have complained.

Yes, it was frustrating, especially because my hubby was definitely a great catch. For a girl who wanted a Fwb, with no strings attached, he was a prize. Plus, with fancy meals and hotels, I wished I could have that too.

"I don't need fancy," I said. The guys were really lucky. They didn't have to hide their dirty thoughts because I started off talking about sex.

I was a cougar and I had needs. But, I was also looking for a friend with benefits. Sex wasn't enough. I had dreams and games to play. Like any girl on the app, I was looking for a match. So first, I had to shed that adultress virgin flower.

I was scared.

I didn't have much of a hook up period. Maybe, two months of dates and at most a few kisses in between high school and college.

Over twenty years of sleeping with the same man, knowing how to please him, I was still nervous. I wasn't sure if I could let myself go or have a stranger man touch me. Even though I had many naughty experiences online and saw tens of guys jerking off and cumming in front of the camera at me, this was definitely different.

Yes, this baby cougar was a pussy cat. A coward. Inexperienced. It was easy to be sexy and confident online.

After chatting with strangers from the apps, I narrowed it down to two men. Both guys fell into my type bracket to the T:

East Asian, between the ages of 25-35 (at that time, it was my range, and okay, the 24-year-old was slightly off range, but I wanted my cherry popped. I knew that if I didn't do this, I wouldn't be able to move on and try the things I wanted to try once I got to Korea.

I had a rep to maintain. Online, I was the wild, sensual Milf cougar, the hot, experienced woman — the dream lover of every man wanting a mature woman in his bed. I couldn't be that virginal girl. It would be embarrassing.

The 24-year-old was an American-born Chinese guy from the city. He was 6 feet 4, fit, liked sports, and talked a lot. He was overly confident and worked in a VC.

34 yo was a Taiwanese guy, an easy-going, friendly, jokey, intelligent guy who could switch conversations from light-hearted to deep, thoughtful words. His name is K.

Both were good-looking, experienced, and ready.

"I know this is a selfish request. We just started talking, but I was just wondering if we could do a video call or a meetup? I'm about to do a vid call with a guy, and if it goes well, I will meet him on Saturday, and we might do it," I said.

"We could hang out sometime this weekend? What's your schedule like?" K asked.

I was stressed about it — my adulterous virginity. My heart was hammering in my chest. This was beginning to feel more like a hammer breaking glass.

"It will be my first time having sex with another guy in 20 years. Wanna make sure that guy is someone I really like. Not just someone who popped my cherry."

"I got it. Let's have a 3-way meetup lol. Jk," K said. "Perhaps we can hang out later that day? Unless things go really well for you two. No pressure."

"Omg. That would be awkward. Much as 3some is on my bucket list. No."

"So your 3some goal is 2m 1f?" K asked. "I had a 2f 1m exp. Didn't go as I planned, haha."

"What happened?" I asked.

"The two ladies are best friends, and they called a timeout halfway to address their jealousy/friendship issues. I sat there being an audience."

"Are you for real?" I laughed.

It was f-ing hilarious. I imagine him sitting there naked and frustrated. The age-old dilemma that any guy would hate — two women fighting.

He wasn't the first. Another guy had told me of how his three-some failed, too. Women were a sensitive breed, and the egos of guys made male-male-female threesome not a fun situation to be in, either.

But those dreams will have to wait.

"Things are much funnier when we look back," he said.

I totally agreed. All experience is worth having — the good, the bad, the ugly.

And so I chose him. K, the guy who failed at three-soming. Just before we were supposed to meet that weekend, he caught Covid. For three to four weeks, we chatted, exchanged naughty pics, and had phone sex.

It felt right, and despite not seeing more of his pics, and only one before he got sick, I was getting excited to finally meet him. After a bad case of Covid and a cold, he was finally healthy again.

"H said get a good hotel. No motels or three stars," I told K.

"Hahaha. No pressure," K replied.

Maybe, there was a tiny bit of expectation.

It was the day after my birthday. It was a new year, a new lover, and we were meeting clandestinely in a hotel.

I was following a stranger to a strange room.

My heart was racing. One foot into the hotel lobby. I could still turn and run.

"Hi," he said, and I swiveled around.

K wasn't exactly what I had pictured him to be when I saw his photograph. I have learned by now that cameras taken at different angles give different pictures. Though K was going to be my first, he wasn't the first person I met. That one, V, would be in another story about swingers and cucks.

"Hey," I glanced at him again quickly. He was wearing a pull-over branded white hoodie and jeans. Sunglasses, looking casual and cool.

I was wearing a long-sleeved white cut-out blouse at the top of my breasts and tight blue jeans. Under my killer attack was dark rose-pink laced lingerie — a half-cupped bra, matching garters, sexy T-panty, and black stockings, hidden by my knee-high boots.

In the elevator, he moved in. Standing so close to me, our arms brushed while I glanced everywhere, everything except him.

"This is my first time doing this in a hotel," he said.

I looked up at him. He had nice coffee-brown eyes and a friendly demeanor. He reached down and held my hand. Unlike H, he wasn't super tall, maybe half a head taller than me.

His warm fingers crossed with mine, and with the heat of his breath on my hair, I felt more relaxed.

He pulled me out when the elevator door opened, and we hurried through the dark, burgundy hallway. I briefly remembered some gold fixtures before he flashed the card key and pulled me into the hotel room.

He dropped his hand, and I walked further into the lion's den. The room was dark with shades drawn, a large King-sized bed on my right with white linen, and a large TV on a walnut dresser on my right.

I dropped my bag on the dresser and felt him behind me.

"Am I what you expect?" he asked in his low, smooth voice.

That was one of the reasons why I picked him. It seemed all women liked smooth voices. Height, intelligence, broad shoulders, muscled arms, washboard abs, and strong thighs were nature's way of selecting the perfect male.

In my case, I already had my forever male, partner-in-crime, hot Big Boss daddy — H, and we have populated the world with our descendants. Now, Yolo-ing was fun, extra gravy, and lots better. It was new and a thrill. The unexpected was an aphrodisiac.

K was so close, standing behind me, helping me off my coat. One hand on my shoulder and the other on my waist. He pulled me into him, his body smashing into mine as I felt his erection eagerly pushing against the curve of my ass.

My hands went back and wrapped around his body so I'd not fall. His lips were on my neck, hot breath in my hair.

"I want you so much. You are such a tease," he said. "I hated being sick when I couldn't touch you."

I turned around, and his lips locked into mine. Soft and then firm as he pushed his tongue between my teeth. I kissed him back hard, sucking at his bottom lip as he growled, pulling me tight into him.

His hands were squeezing my arms and then dropping down to my ass and cupping as much as he could, his fingers running up to my waist and to the button and zipper of my jeans.

"Take it off," he ordered and pushed me down onto the bed.

I fell with a "plop" sound, the bed bounced back as he dropped onto me, blocking my escape. His mouth landed on my neck, his tongue licking as he tasted my sweat and breathed in my nervousness.

"You okay?" he asked, slowly backing up as he caught my shifty eyes. I locked my gaze on his dilated eyes, aroused and ready to eat me whole.

"Sorry, I can't help myself," he said. "I'll go to the bathroom. You take your time."

I watched him walk away and sat up on the bed. This was it.

By the end of today, this would be a new me. A road once taken could never return.

Was I ready? If not now, when?

Twenty years flashed in a blink. The years of change from the sweet-innocence, somewhat rebellious teen of college years to the young adult entering the world of work, the woman who became a mother, a mother struggling with a crying child and endless ups and downs of family life, insecurities, low self-esteem, second child, marriage on thin ropes and Covid, losing loved ones, a health scare and finally here.

Dirty, naughty, Milf, bombshell. The new budding me. A rose, thorny and seconds to deflowering. Heart hammering in my chest.

There was no going back. I didn't want to either. So much promise was at stake. Adventures awaited them, as it was now.

I heard the rush of water as I unzipped my jeans. My garter slipped out as I arranged the straps on my thighs. I took off my boots, smoothed out my black lace stockings, pulled off my white blouse, and arranged my dark rose bra, taut nipples peeking out.

I took a deep breath.

"Ready?" I heard him calling from the bathroom.

I climbed onto the bed on my knees. Shoulders arched, back bent, pearl-white smooth ass facing up, and turned to him as he walked out.

"Holy…" He stopped, and I watched his mouth drop.

"Hi." My voice was low and sultry, my smile showing my teeth.

This cougar was ready.

My three-year Yolo stint in the world beyond had taught me a few things. One, not to be burdened by the actions of others, and that guilt which came with cheating lay in the hands of the one who cheated. If not me, then someone else.

Second, trust was of the utmost importance in an Open relationship. In our case, we had our decades of friendship, love, and family bonds. Jealousy did creep in. If you don't love, you won't be jealous. But these days, jealousy came in the form of me getting more experiences, meeting different guys, while he had loads of fun with his Fwbs, while I was still searching and securing mine.

A relationship was about owning. The vows taken basically handed you the right to molest your spouse as much as you want. My hand loved reaching forward and landing on hot skin and muscles. A man's shoulders, arms, abs, and butt — smooth, silky, and hard.

There was no doubt I am a perv. Now, through the apps and meets, I had access to more hot young men than I could ever imagine. All consensual and eager to experience a Milf and pick up a skill or two.

My fingers brushing a new guy's arms, shoulders, and then slowly trailing down, following his taut nipples, endless ridges of chocolate ribs, and muscles.

It was a two-way street; the guys got to touch as I did.

Thrills and feels.

Watching him shudder the moment I grabbed him. Squeezing him in my hand. The look in his eyes as he watched me staring at him, hungrily devouring all of him as he pounded my screams out.

The echoes of my voice bounced off the walls, sweat sticky, and the scent of lust. The road I took was laying paths in the sand. Carving out the woman I became.

CHAPTER FIVE

BABY COUGAR AND HER WOLF CUBS

DOMME-ME-NO EFFECT

"He wants to be squashed like a bug and caged like an animal."

His name is Al, and he liked Dommes and got a kick out of being ordered around. Being a Domme wasn't my thing. As a cougar, I enjoyed pouncing on my young fish, but at the end of the fight, the switch was what I loved.

I didn't think much when Al and I started chatting. I was on a new local dating app — Hinge, which focused on matching singles looking to get hitched.

Marrying wasn't a possibility, so I had to be creative. I didn't want to lie to the guys on the app, and if it were Bumble or Tinder, I would have stated my intentions clearly.

We made a bet I'd not get a fish to bite if I didn't list I was looking for a friend with benefits. Was it true that all men on the apps were after sex? Was I not worth chasing if I didn't put myself out for fun and sex?

This was a test I had to find out.

"Forget MBTI. Choose Boobs or Butt? Which are you?"

I couldn't help myself. I am naughty and loved my words. My profile had to be unique, naughty, and spicy. No pics in lingerie, but my word craft spoke louder.

This was why I was shadow-banned from Tinder. Yes, that Tinder – the one app that nudes probably could pass censors without a blink of an eye. But it wasn't the nudes that got me in trouble.

It was a dirty poem.

I wrote the prose in English and translated it into Korean because I thought Tinder bots weren't smart enough to translate a picture written in Korean as something naughty.

The one thing I never considered was the human element. A jilted Korean fish-to-be hated that I didn't pick him, flagged me and had me secretly shadow banned.

And so I digressed again, back to our favorite Submissive Al.

Al seemed normal enough—a typical Asian American engineer in the Valley of Engineers.

Al's type of Asian story was common – an Asian immigrant family, first or second gen. Middle income. With unlimited expectations such as getting grades As, AP and honor classes, piano playing, Science, Math, and Spelling bees, and Chinese after school, and other weekend sports and STEM learning. Hanging out with other Asian pals, going to Ivy League or Stanford, Berkeley, or UCLA, and then finding a programming job in the valley.

His age was 27, within my age range - having worked a few years and being the young, virile, and horny type who could keep going. However, I learned my hunger for sex was still too much for these guys.

With his boyish looks, Al is cuter than most. You would never suspect the dirty boy with that outward facade. And, unlike the others, last year when we first spoke, Al approached me from a different point of attack — seeking instead to learn how to cook.

I loved to cook and was a huge foodie. I couldn't resist helping. He was living alone and needed some skills to survive. Call it mama instincts, food instincts, or hungry hungry cougar. I was caught. Smart guy.

We were supposed to meet at a park. Maybe play a little in the car to get a feel of each other. But our first meeting in the park didn't happen because he pulled out first.

"Sorry. I can't meet. I have a girlfriend now," he said. "We agreed to date online first."

"Okay…" I wasn't shocked. A little disappointed. Some of the guys I chatted with or met had significant others or wives. The other half might have girls they were meeting and dating. The rest were single and liked things unattached. Online chatting didn't transcend into commitment, and I wanted no restraint, so I expected them to like the freedom our open chat and sex gave.

Talking to Al caught up again after I returned from Asia one year later. It was October, and he told a secret I never thought I'd hear.

"My first meetings are in coffee shops. I won't want to be trapped in a guy's house," I said.

"Yeah…I know how that feels. I was almost trapped once," Al replied.

"Huh? A girl blocked your way? How?" Al was six feet. Not bulky but definitely not easy to overcome.

"Not a girl. A guy," he said.

"Whoa…wait, what? Guy? What…what are you doing with a guy?" The last time I knew from chatting with him, he was straight, not bisexual. Al liked girls. He liked girl parts very much. He enjoyed my Insta updates, and we traded vids of us masturbating.

"I was going to give him a blow job," he texted it so casually.

"Omg! Whhhhyy?" I forgot to breathe. This was insane.

"My Domme ordered me to do it."

"The girl in London? Your girlfriend?"

"Yes…" He added a smiley face.

"Whyyyy?"

"She wanted me to suck cock, and I had to film it."

My jaw dropped. Literally, I seriously didn't know what to say. Flabbergasted. I had to tell someone.

"He sucked dicks!" I texted to my online guy pals.

"Oh my god! He sucks cock for his Domme!" I spoke in hush tones to myself. My face was flushed with excitement.

"Who?" the messages popped up like light bulbs.

"Because his Domme told him to do it, and told him to film it!!"

There was something freeing about our conversations. Sex broke those barriers.

I jumped onto the bed and continued texting.

"And so you did it?" I asked Al, trying to hold back my excitement. Didn't want to scare my fish away.

"Not with that guy," he replied.

"Why? U said he cornered u."

"He did. This guy was big and aggressive. Intense. I don't like guys, but I was attracted to him."

"Really? Why?"

"He was a real Dom. He wanted me to suck him. I like that kind of energy."

"So you mean that's sexy? So it's to be dominated that you like?"

"I like the intensity, but I didn't feel like it…," he said.

"He must be upset that you changed your mind," I said.

"Yeah."

"So what did you tell your Domme?"

"I told her I'd find someone else…" he said.

"Where do you find these men?"

I was still shocked by the idea of Al sucking a man's penis. I agree, I'm not as flexible as I should be, but it was just unexpected after all the flirting and playing we did together, and him not showing up in my gaydar.

"Sometimes Tinder, Grindr, or Twitter," he said.

"Did you have sex with them?"

"Definitely not. I'm not into guys," he said.

"But you suck their cocks," I replied.

"That's when I was okay with them. I don't do that now."

"I'm confused," I said.

"I do what my Domme tells me, but I also draw the line."

"So sex is drawing the line?"

"Yeah…" he said.

Mind you, our conversations were based on my memory and could be somewhat fictitious because I lost our convos when I deleted my Line app. Still, the gist was there. Our Al was a major Domme boy.

And he wasn't the first I'd spoken to.

"He gets high on control. He wanna be squashed like a bug and caged like an animal. It thrills him that his Domme hasn't come to see him. She keeps changing the dates, and that makes him more excited." I told my friends.

Submissives came in all shapes, forms, ages, and races. Unlike Al, I'd be the first to rebel if a Dom ordered me to eat a pussy out. There would be no way to hell I'd do that. And unlike other subs, I did what I wanted and would rather get punished than do something I didn't want.

"What is your safe word?" Some would ask when they saw me pull out my collar, leash, whip, and cuffs from my toy bag.

Seventy percent of the guys I met in person had never done this. I liked to pick the ones who were pervs in mind but not in body. Young but ready to explore, ready to fuck a Milf and play with a cougar.

I was on their bucket list — a dream come true. They would never get a chance like ever again. And likewise, they were mine.

I won't deny I feel the grains of sand slipping through my fingers. Every day seemed to stretch shorter. There was no other time. If I had to conquer many to feed their needs and mine in only a week, that might be the only way. Why wait for pleasure when you can count your chicks right now? We have already waited a year to meet in Seoul.

There was no better day than today. Who knew what tomorrow brought? Happiness should be wrought in our own hands, and fuck what people say. Why? Despite our age, we were adults in this room.

—oo—

COSPLAY

—oo—

I loved watching them.

The way their hands moved up and down their pink cocks. Sometimes wet from pre-cum glistening like morning dew. Their nicely pale sculpted chests heaving as waves of ecstasy hit their bodies.

And it worked both ways.

I wore my Vicky S laced lingerie in blacks, reds, and greens, depending on my mood. A short silk robe tied with a sash. A light dash of makeup, natural lipstick, and a fluff to my hair, giving an after-bed-sex look, and I was ready.

The ring of loading dots blinked as I waited. And then I was let into the arena. My left fingers were eager to click on the "Stop" when I caught a glimpse of someone I didn't want, and then it was back to "Start" again. The hunt was on, and the prize was a fistful of pleasure buds coursing through my body and his.

That was when I met him — Cosplay guy.

He was hiding behind the screen — Meek like a doe afraid of headlights.

It was another day on Ome where I hunted for my fish. Two months since we went open, and I was having my morning sex play. I had Mondays to Wednesdays mornings because my time in the US vs. Korea meant some were still awake at 1:30 am. And if I missed them, I would catch them awake later with their morning hards around 3 pm my time.

This was a never-ending thirst. A drug of orgasms and the highs that made me want more. Most days, I was doing two, and on good days, maybe three.

Cosplay was a chef and restaurant owner. He cooked and ran his own shop, and barely had time to rest. His only break was a day off on a Tuesday in a month. Every day, he sloughed away. His most popular dish was Kimchi bokkeumbap and pasta. His business was so successful that he had people working for him.

He was twenty-three. A young boss. A Master. And he loved older women. In fact, that was what he said right from the start.

"I love older women."

"You do?" I asked.

"You are very beautiful. I love your smile, your body...your breasts, your ass."

Silky words came pouring out of his mouth as I slowly stripped. I didn't have to ask him. In the Korean dead of night, and in my room with the dark shades drawn, lust rose like dancing fumes. Our sinful thoughts were singing with only one thing in mind.

He knew what to do. His phone dropped from that quick glimpse of his face to his chest, traveling down slowly as my hands did on my body. My eyes followed his camera as it went down lower and lower to his rod, which he was holding in his hand.

Hard, pink, circumcised, as most are. A commonality among Gen Zs. Pulsating like a rolling pin in his hand, ready to burst into seeds.

I giggled, my eyes glinting, or as the guys often say, shining brightly like stars.

"Do you want to see what's under here?" I asked, bending

closer to the laptop as my breasts hung like heavy fruit from my laced bra. Swinging like pendulums snapping in rhythm.

I was past trying to speak in Korean. My actions spoke louder, as he pumped hard, and even faster when my robe slid off my shoulder like water sliding off smooth rock, and pooling on the bed.

I reached over and picked up my purple dildo.

"Eat it," he said.

I giggled again and licked the tip of my hard rubber dildo. He sucked in and ran his fingers down his shaft and up again. I put my mouth on the head and took the entire thing in my mouth, pulling up, revealing a wet path of spit as my tongue licked the wetness from the toy.

He groaned, and I did it again, kissing the head of the dildo and mouth taking down to the base and up again. Sucking a dildo took skill, mimicking his motions with my mouth, him groaning as I moaned and sucked.

"I studied how to give blow jobs," I told him.

"How?" He asked.

"Online. Videos. Read up. Educational videos." I said.

"Huh. Like a sex education vid?" He asked.

"And practiced a lot," I laughed. I wanted to be a better blower. Making the guys I played with excited and explode, was a heady experience.

"Show me your pussy," Cosplay ordered.

"What is your kink?" I asked.

"Maids," he said. "I like all maid costumes. All costumes — nurse, doctor, police, all costumes."

"Cosplay," I said. "You like cosplay." Cool and quiet. He barely spoke and watched quietly with an intense gaze. It was easier to open a clam than his mouth.

He had nice lips. A boyish face with large doe eyes, unlike most Koreans. A cool haircut and the confidence of someone who ran his own business.

"How old are you?" I asked.

"What does it matter? I like you a lot. You are so beautiful, and I want to play with you for a long time."

"So, you want to be my Fwb?" I asked.

"Yes," he said.

"Don't you play with other girls?" I asked.

"You have many guys."

"True, I do," I smiled.

"But, I like you the most," he said.

"Okay, let's be Fwb." And that was how it started. He was my first online Friend with benefits. We weren't just friends. He had seen all my privates and closed up and far.

"Show me," he said, and I pointed my phone at my wetness after a round of orgasm that he caused by pumping his stick so well and his cold instructions of what he wanted me to do.

"Open your legs," he ordered.

I sat on the ground and opened in the W-shape that they all liked.

"Put it in," he said. "Harder...faster..."

I did as he told, and in seconds, he watched as I orgasmed. With him, I did it again and again, listening to his groans and moans, and watching him play but not cumming.

"Why don't you cum?" I asked, panting, staring at the river of squirt flowing down and under my bed.

I was a dirty bitch.

He laughed. I caught his eyes twinkling as he stared at me. "I like you too much. I don't want to cum. I'm holding back."

"Do you ever cum?" I asked.

A good question. He never cummed. He stayed hard, and we played an hour or more, leaving me exhausted with the different positions he ordered, while he pumped away and did not cumming.

"I cum," he said.

"When am I going to see it? You know I love cum." I pouted.

Yes. That was part of the reason the vid calls drove me wild. The ending, the satisfaction of getting the guy off. The sound of his final climax as mine came straight after.

He laughed. "You'll see when we meet. And if you want it, tell me. I will play with you."

But things never turned out the way we wanted. We promised to meet every Tuesday morning to play, but he only made it three times and then stopped.

I wore new lingerie each time we met, and being new to this, I practiced how I'd seduce him. We played stripping, which I loved, and he laughed at my shyness even after he'd seen everything.

With him, our vid call was always an hour, and I orgasmed four times and squirted twice each time we met. He knew how to extend our play and loved watching me.

"I want to see your face," he said. "You're so beautiful when you cum."

And then one day he disappeared. Two weeks went by, and I waited like a love-lost girl by the laptop. Waiting for him to show. I figured he was busy with work and exhausted. I was worried he fell sick, and there was no way other than from Insta and Kakao to reach him.

We weren't close.

We were just sex friends.

We weren't Fwbs. I was just bluffing myself.

The black silky bodysuit that I wore the day Cosplay ghosted me didn't go to waste. I filmed my doggy acts. My moans and cries mixed with lust and sadness. My breasts escaped as I moved.

I am the Milf. I am the Cougar.

The Cougar didn't cry. She hunted. She is Queen.

And that was how my first Fwb ended. Or so I thought.

—oo—

MAIDO FRAIDO

—oo—

There are memes of them everywhere. Men in maid costumes, some big and hairy, slim and effeminate, and others muscled, hot bods in silly frilly outfits, just for laughs.

He wore that and sent it to me. The dangerously hot guy I saw on Bumble, and I thought there was no way he was real. Hotter and more handsome than some of the K-pop guys we all know — perfect Korean hairstyles with trimmed black brows, beautiful monoids, high-bridged nose, sensual lips, and sharp jawline. He could be the poster boy for those Korean beauty surgery ads we see along Seoul subways and billboards, cos let's face it, even the K guys are going under the knife these days.

Perhaps talking about sex and sharing naughty pics did open more doors. Letting out the beasts and quirks these men had to hide in an Asian society where first impressions make or break.

He chose me first on Bumble, and I responded, a little surprised that he was into me.

"I love Milfs," he messaged.

"Annyeong, hello :)" I replied. Yes, cliche to use Korean mixed with English, but I was a foreigner despite my East Asian skin color, and I am learning Korean.

"You have big boobs. I love boobs," he continued. "I'm HK," he said. "Let's chat on Insta."

And that was how we met online, and how everything started.

Hot guy, as I called him and named him so H, my husband, knew, was almost lust-perfect. The stats in his profile showed he was in his late twenties, working, tall at six feet, and loved to eat and watch anime, and was into scifi. Later, I learned we shared the same book types and loved to travel. And most of all, he was a great big perv. One of the most Byeontae of my catch.

He had an Insta page for all the women, Milfs, and Cougars he caught with his super racy, nude shots, which for sure turned every woman to jelly each time he posted. His lean, muscled body, smooth skin, broad shoulders, and underpants riding low to a big piece, was insane. And one pic of him in underwear had his head peeping out. Seriously, was that legal on Insta?

"Do you have an OF?" I asked once. "Your pics are really good. I bet you can get lots of views."

I've seen my share of naughty pics on Insta. Those hot Asian guys and their muscled bods in poses to attract an ultimate number of foreign pussies, were unfairly posted everywhere, whereas my few pics of my barely covered boobs got censored the second I uploaded.

Lately, I've been thinking Insta was on to me. Those AI bots were watching my every move and waiting eagerly to take me down. It was a little more than too unfair when I knew for a fact that there were other accounts with more sleazier pics and women and men getting away with advertising their wares for their OF and porn pages.

I am a writer. And so what if I dabbled in a little show-and-tell? A Milf Cougar needs to have a little fun. And my fish have to be fed. They, too, needed some love and attention, right?

Back to Hotguy. I thought it was interesting that on his Insta account, he stated he was a "Voice, audio lover". What was that? Because at first, when I was chatting with him, I thought, yes, he was hot, but there are hot guys everywhere. It was curiosity that got me to him because he was placing voice before looks.

"What sounds do you like to hear?" I asked.

"Voices," he said.

"Do voices make you horny?" I asked.

"Some do. Can I call you?" he asked.

"Sure."

And so he did. The call was voice-only. Step by step, we talked dirty.

He spoke with a little broken English, and I was lost in my lust, imagining the guy in the pics doing dirty on me. Rubbing myself and showing him my boobs unfairly cos I turned my vid on and he didn't. I preferred video chat because it gave me the chance to check the goods and catch a catfish earlier.

To be honest, his voice wasn't what I'd expected from his looks. I wondered if it was a habit. My imagination and expectations don't match. Often, the guys with attractive voices I talked to weren't as visually stunning. Maybe voices gave the normal guys their extra leg up.

Maybe in our Internet age, we are giving ourselves more chances. With AI, online RPG games, Avatars, voices, and texting, we are no longer judging people only by the way they look. After a year of chatting, did each person stand a bigger chance of finding their perfect match?

Sure. Maybe. And that's happily ever after. Or when friends, colleagues, and acquaintances gossip and say — How on earth did he or she level up? You'd feel a sense of pride.

To each his or her own, right? Your hotter partner could be lacking in something else that you could give.

The Kdrama tropes of Cinderella or Frog Prince meeting their rich, handsome Cheobol guy, a beautiful woman, while playing online games and becoming online lovers despite societal norms. Good luck dreaming that. Reality is 96% not happening. Sorry to burst your bubble. And for a Milf Cougar, like myself, this whole happily ever after wasn't what I wanted.

I'm in it for LUST, not LOVE.

Objectification is Number 1. Settling for anything less is just selling out on my part, pity friend sex, and just blindingly horny at the moment that I'll hump a lamppost.

It doesn't matter how I look. I had what that guy needed and lusted for. In such situations, I was confident enough to know I'm going to jump a hot, young guy and he'd remember how awesome it was.

So what if I was older, curvier, and not as pretty as those young Asian dolls? I was going to blow his mind like he was going to blow mine.

The first voice sex with Hot guy HK was fun, despite his higher-pitched voice.

I had distinct likes — his voice was mid-to-low range. I like my men not to sound like they are girls when they cum, and to grunt and moan like a man who had just ejaculated into my tight, warm cave with a grip that wasn't going to let him go till I milked him completely dry.

After many lessons learned, these virile young men with all-night stamina were total bullshit. Or maybe I've attracted too many stressed-out, tired men, who can't make it past 2 am.

Hot guy HK had me dreaming. His telling me of the moms he'd taken and how he liked to do it and sending me videos of him jerking off only made it hard to concentrate. His sext vids were the ones I watched the most, and when I needed release and couldn't find a guy online to play with, and was too lazy to meet new people, he was my go-to vid. Getting me to cum in under three minutes by re-running his vids close to five times.

My favorite vid was the one where he was sitting at the edge of a tub, naked in his young man splendor and being edged and jerked off by an older woman dressed in a sweater and pants.

It was the consistent motion of her hand, gripping his rod hard, slippery with the sound of oily wetness and the catch in his voice as he tried to hold back his moans and gasps. I never got to see if he came. He had other videos of those special times. But the sound of his low voice, repressed as he tried not to cum, was beyond addictive.

I wanted to be that hand. I knew I could do at least three times better. I want to be the woman who gets to jump on that long, thick, hard shaft and feel his warm seed finally ejaculating because my vagina was too tight and wet, and my chest was smothering his face too much; he could no longer hold back.

And that would just be the beginning of us making out all night long.

And Hotguy had to spoil it all with that stupid first maid-costume pic.

"Why did you send that?" I asked. The pic he sent was him in a black and white frilled maid dress with its hem above his knees on his hard, tanned thighs.

His body was smooth, muscled, lean, with chocolate abs and

long legs. His stomach ridges were crazy. He had a bodyscape for hands and lips to roll up and down from the tip of his ear, down his neck, to his wide shoulders, taut nipples, and down and down, you get my gist. Yum.

And then that maid costume. Damn him.

"Why are you sending me this?" I asked again. Pissed that he was breaking my fantasy. All the fun I had with him and with myself, because of this one act, seemed dumb right now.

His perversion had tipped over. No long, hard erection looks good with frills.

"It's a joke for my friends," he said.

"A joke?" My brows were pinched tight, and I was trying not to scream, not from excitement but from annoyance that I had to return to square one to find my perfect lust partner. We had already talked about meeting that coming summer and booking a hotel room on the same floor with my family so he could feel he was cuckolding H. That was his fantasy, but I was willing to follow along if that meant I got to see him.

He showed me a screenshot of his friends in his online game, with their faces blurred, and that maid pic he sent them.

Fine. Be childish. Okay, I let it pass. We had a few more encounters because he kept calling to hear my orgasm voice, and I left him my orgasm voice after masturbating to his vids and pics, making him super horny. He loved that, and I was excited after seeing him being sucked by girls and wanting to do the same for him.

Something was up. The red flags were growing day by day.

"Why don't we vid sex?" I asked him. I knew he was cumming because I could hear him, but that Summer passed, and when I was in Seoul, we didn't meet. He couldn't take the train to Seoul and had to work. And then he asked a weird question. One, which if I tell H, he would say abort at once.

I wished this were the story I had told him with happy memories. There will be other stories about Hotguy. There was too much history between us not to write a few. But for now, I'm talking about maids, and he wasn't the only one who had a maid fetish in that weird way. For those guys, I'd asked why, and one guy said he was bi, and his maid cosplays was one of the reasons why I didn't speak to him for a year. After finally meeting, the sex was awesome.

As for Hotguy again, that wasn't the last maid pic he sent. Once in a while, he'd drop one on me, and each time, it took me days and weeks to get over them. Those maid pics did damage. For Hotguy, masturbating in that dress and shooting cum with those frills around him was almost hard to swallow.

"You are not open-minded," someone said.

"Yeah. I'm not. I'm Open, but I'm not open-minded," I replied. At this point, after two years, this is me. I am who I am. Curious about sex, but have a strong taste and type for what I like.

Life is short.

The big bang dream will come when the time comes. Weirdo, maido, or whatever. I won't be afraid.

Because I'm the queen. And a cougar roars when she roars.

—oo—

KISS LIKE KDRAMA

—oo—

He came from a distance. Tall, mysterious, Korean. Every K-drama girl's dream came true. White shirt tucked neatly, long tapered black pants: broad shoulders, clean Korean-styled hair.

Heart thudding hard in my chest. I stood conflicted by my car. Was this what I wanted?

Flashback, hours to the night before this fateful day.

We met online on a dating app. It was serendipitous because during the month or so I'd been on, I had never seen a Korean guy in the dating cards. Swiping left mostly and giving up at the ten thousand likes. No way I was gonna be able to go through the piles of White, Latino, Black, Indians, and a bunch of other guys whom I didn't care for.

Yes, I am a sex racist. Don't you shake your brows at me. Sex was the only thing I could proudly say, I'm a racist. We all had the right to choose who to fuck. So there.

So when this guy who was my type appeared, you could imagine my excitement. Within seconds after a few messages, I learned he had a girlfriend. Downer. Just to be clear, I tried not to mess with guys in relationships. However, there were exceptions, like this case.

Plus, he knew I was married and Open. This wasn't a romance but a hookup in broad daylight with the noon sun bearing down on us.

Yes, it was hot. The sun was scorching hot.

Little beads of sweat were trickling down the side of my face as I tried to shade my eyes from the glare of the disapproving star.

I came this far. This was my chance to test it out.

Test what you ask? Test my nerves because I was going to Seoul — the city of my dreams, in a month and a half. Seoul, my Dizzyland, where this cougar's goal was gotta-catch-them-all, Korean mice.

Was this baby big cat ready?

Every guy who spoke to me would know I have a bit of a fetish. Okay, more than a bit — a disease called 'Yellow fever'.

Who said Yellow fever was only for those not yellow? Okay, so I had a thing for Koreans. Blame Kpop, and Kdrama. The wave came and left me lost and desperate. I had to do this. Call it purging. Eat till I surfeited. As for objectification, it worked both ways. They loved my Milfy curves, and I loved their looks.

"I'm trying to prove a point," I said. "Research. Stories for my book. Yolo journey..."

Seoul guy was here for a week in April, on a business training trip. Last night was his only chance to hook up before returning to his native soil. He wanted a taste of American girls, and lucky for him, he hooked up with an Asian American Milf. Lucky for me, I thought I was chatting with a cute, twenty-six-year-old Korean guy.

If things went as planned. Some kissing, some pawing, and maybe a little more. Back then, I was a newbie. Rules were made as we went. H and I had road bumps, but still, we were speeding ahead.

My desert was dry, and I was determined to live life to the

fullest. Covid taught us, in a snap, that things could end. We would not regret. I would not regret. I was gonna leave a mark. A memory for those seeking meaning in their lives. I was there. I made them happy even for the briefest of moments as they made miine.

I exited the highway. At that point, I chickened out and told H. The meeting point with the Seoul guy was a coffee shop near his hotel. In a few hours, he'd be on a plane heading back to shining Dizzyland.

"Meet him," H said. "Have no regrets."

Having had my first stranger sex under my belt, I pushed myself forward. This was different. The K boys I met were online. Online sex was being done in the dark. A ray of lust-filled satisfaction. The lack of communication made the fun mysterious and all the more thrilling.

Would it be the same?

I was minutes from the coffee shop. Another message popped up.

"I don't have the car. I can't meet at the coffee shop," he said.

"What? Where do you want to meet?" I asked.

"How about the hotel?" he asked.

"What?" Red flags were ringing. I was pulling over and texting. This guy was suspicious. I was ready to call it a day.

If I didn't meet another Korean before I leave for Seoul would I be okay?

It took me days to plan my schedule in Seoul – which guy I should meet on which day, and going so far as to pick my lingerie for each guy based on their likes and dislikes. My naughty suitcase was laid out, and the toys were put in. I was ready to raze the ground, blazing in perverted glory.

But, everything was just a thought-out idea. All would fail if I bailed out. What would happen if the first Korean guy I saw gave me a severe case of anxiety? Couldn't perform? Endless tearing up? Who knew what I might do? Stuttering? An experiment was needed for this closeted big cat.

When I got to his hotel, the guy sent me another message saying I should get a room. He had two hours before leaving for the airport, and his excuse was that his boss and colleagues were in the same hotel, and he couldn't be seen meeting a woman there.

The warnings were flapping in the wind. It took a thirty-minute drive to meet him, and I was determined to do what I set out to do. Hell and wildfire.

"No. I'm not getting a room," I said firmly.

"Okay, how about the parking lot? I checked, and no one is there," he said.

"Parking lot?" I got out of my car. I'd parked at the hotel and took a quick look around. He was right. There wasn't anyone. Flanked by the highway, putting range, and an office building, the Saturday lot was empty.

"Okay, fine. See you there," I said.

I chose the furthest spot I could find amid the roaring of cars and the constant popping sounds of balls.

"I'm coming out," he said.

What was I doing? Funny, sexy, and weird. My life wasn't the norm anymore. Stories of my encounters brewed, the sex tales these stranger guys told, thoughts dripping as the tsunami in my head grew.

Was this what I wanted?

The guy was walking towards me, and I to him. The distance edged closer and closer, minute by minute, each breath, each beating heart.

Wait. Who is this? I stopped.

He came the rest of the way.

"Is that you?" I asked first. 'You' because I really forgot his name, and because I am still shocked at this point. I'm reliving the K-drama moment when the spark fizzled. When the male lead turned into the spare actor in the background.

"You look different," I spoke again because he didn't.

"You look the same," he smiled. "So pretty."

My insides cringed. Oh. My. God.

"You don't look the same," I replied. How was I supposed to repeat it without sounding rude?

He was waiting, and I looked away, and then caught his eyes again, which were smiling, too. Obviously, he liked what he saw.

I was dressed to seduce in a brown one-piece body-hugging knitted dress with a low V-cut neckline.

"You bulked up." I finally spoke again. His face was the first thing I noticed. It wasn't sharp, and his whole body was twice as big as it was in his profile pictures.

"You like it?" He flexed his arm, and his bicep popped. He came really close now.

I turned to my car and started walking briskly away while he followed. "That's my car." I pointed stupidly at the only vehicle in the entire parking lot.

My stomach was churning. He wasn't bad-looking, but I was built on expectations, especially when I had a game play thought out, only to have my rug pulled from under me.

The words were drilled into my head. "You can't back down. Think of the guys in Seoul."

Yes, this was my pre-test.

I can talk to him. I can flirt. I can get what I want and make this fun.

When we arrived at my car, I swiveled around and side-stepped him. Korean guy backed into my car, leaning against it, as he peered down at me. At six feet over, he was a head taller than me.

And then, in a Kdrama move, I tiptoed and slammed my right palm on the car, beside his ear, then stretched my arm out. His brows lifted in confusion. And then, I smashed my lips onto his.

He smelt like cigarettes.

Too late.

He grabbed my head and kissed me back hard, holding onto the back of my head, as his tongue swirled in my mouth and snatched my tongue every second he caught. His strong arms wrapped around my waist and pulled me against his steel body. Locked in a vise, he kissed me endlessly, as we baked in the heat. Before finally pulling back to gasp for air.

I stared at him, my mouth full of smoke.

"Get into the car," he said.

I coughed. Puffing like a train.

"Okay, you go there." I wrenched my hands and pointed to the front passenger seat, and he looked confused when I marched off to the driver's side.

He was a rhino in the passenger seat.

"Urmm." He scrunched.

"Press that button at the side," I said, and watched him trying to fiddle with the seat button.

He tried to get his seat backward, and got up instead and then the seat twisted and turned.

I climbed over him, got out of the car to the other side through the door and then press the button to adjust for him.

The seat grunted, moving like a conveyor belt, achingly in slow. We stared at the seat and then at each other.

Fate was telling me — "Go home!" As if she knew what was to come and was putting the brakes on the disaster that was about to happen.

This wasn't an In-Lust-With-Him moment. He lost his appeal when I realized he didn't look like his profile pic.

Was I superficial? Yes. Was that a sin? I felt cheated. Catfished. I came expecting one, but I got another instead.

Yet, I stayed. Determined to see this through. Stubbornly wanting my furture Seoul trip to be perfect. My friends in Seoul expected me to be the cougar, not the bunny, in a fox robe.

"Okay," I said.

"Okay," he took a deep breath.

I went back to my driver's side of the car. "Let's start over," I said.

"Over there? On you?" His brow raised. "Not here?" He pointed to his lap.

Dude was not the cleverest of the pod.

My face flushed. "Well. No." I grabbed both sides of my dress.

Show Time. I did not practice it in front of the mirror, but I practiced it several times in my head.

It was all in the wrists. In one swoop, a flip of my hands, I pulled my dress over my head and off.

My boobs popped instead of bunny ears.

"Wow! Wooow," his voice dropped. Hands flashed over and grabbed and massaged my appendages.

I looked up, and our eyes met. I could see his arousal both in his gaze and the bulge in his pants. My red lingerie, with its second-skin smoothness and half-cupped creamy breasts, was magic.

I climbed onto him with his hands on my hips. He buried his head into my breasts and breathed in deeply. Lips kissing and licking my skin, and hungrily reaching for my nipple as his other hand was milking my left breast, and squeezing hard.

He was murmuring. Words of praise, and his other hand dropped to unbuckle his belt and unzip.

"No." I stopped his hand. "No sex."

"Why no?" He muttered between kisses. "I thought this is what you want."

"No. I said we will meet and see how we match, and if we do, we have sex in Seoul."

"But, I want you now," he said. "You're too hot."

His hand reached under my short lingerie dress, like a missile zooming straight for my red T-panty, fingers hooking on the strings, pulling closer, digging down for what was under.

I made a grab for his hand, and his lips were on my throat, and then, when he buried his head into my chest again, as I turned to my left.

A shadow blotched the light. A shark in the shape of a black car, its hood facing straight at us, stared.

"What the Fuck!" I pushed the Korean guy off my chest. His magnetic head latched back on.

"Damn it! Car!" I shouted, pushing him off and pointing.

The black car reversed and pulled up behind my trunk again.

"Cop!" The sky had collapsed. "Cop!" I pushed the guy's head off my breasts.

"Huh?" He looked up, confused. I could tell from his dilated eyes that he was too lust drunk to think.

"The cops are here!" I shouted. Pointing, jabbing at the shark's bonnet, and squinting at the tinted windows of the security car.

I was still on the Korean guy. My movements were waterlogged as I jumped to my driver's seat. Boobs were exposed, but I didn't care. I popped them in my lingerie and turned around to face the cop.

The Korean guy threw my dress on my chest, and as I turned to back out. But the cop car taunted, waiting a few more seconds before relenting.

I raced down the empty car park with the cop chasing after. As I got closer to the Korean guy's hotel, he shouted. "My hotel! I'm flying…"

I slammed the brakes, "Get off!" Glancing at the cop car coming closer. "Hurry! Get off."

Like a teenager mopping, the Korean guy slouched out with his jacket in his hand.

"I'll see you again?" he asked.

"Are you for real?" I glared at him.

"What?" he was confused.

We were in the middle of the parking lot, and a cop car was waiting. In my mind, there was never.

Never again would I do this. Never had a cop car chased me. Never would I forget this day.

I burnt rubber, hell hounds nipping at my feet. I was doing

seventy-five miles per hour on the expressway, not once looking back. I kept on speeding, my heart pounding hard, hammering against my ribs. Two exits later, I checked my rear view.

The cop was gone.

Several miles more, and I exited the highway, found an office building with no camera, and changed.

Never again. That's what I told the next guy I met. A nice doctor who had sex with a nurse in their night shift room. She was hot and had tattoos, he said. The domme nurse pushed him onto the bed, tied him up, and took him.

No. I didn't play with him. I didn't play with the next guy, either. The security car etched in my mind.

I didn't see the cop's face, but he haunted my dreams in that black car. Faceless hunter who haunted my weeks, and then, in a snap, I was back again.

This time I promised to be clever. Lust won.

Years later, and car fun was still a thing. Never say never. Cos, lust was a drug I couldn't resist, and where was a better place than a movable hotel?

Who was I kidding? This milf cougar lived for the thrill.

—o THOUGHTS: o—

The ordinary guy who no one would ever suspect of taking cocks for his Domme, and the silly guy who cummed in a cup for a chance to date. Guys in maid costumes with their privates flying high. Romance scammers and mommy boys with their fantasies hidden tighter than their belts.

Our lives took twists and turns that we wouldn't have thought — rabbit holes, burying deeper as the ground caved in. We chased the rainbows, hoping for a glimpse of something wonderful.

D-day was a beacon, golden light shining bright.

Seoul was a month away — time to face the dream I'd always wanted. Ever since I saw my first K-drama, [Romance of a Bonus Book], I badly wanted it. Somewhere along the way, children came, and my life took a swerve, and those things that I thought were important and fun in my twenties fled by the cries of those who needed me.

The thirties were a time of sacrifice. When I was a teen, I asked my mother if she liked being my mom. "It is my duty," she said.

Her words hurt like a knife through my heart. Looking back a decade after my thirties, those words no longer hurt. Like a cycle, my daughter asked me if I regretted being a mom.

"No, I've no regrets," I told her.

I didn't believe in what-ifs. The journey would always be paved with rocks and roses. Taking a pebble away meant those pebbles that followed didn't exist.

I wasn't my mother.

I am proud of who I am now — curvy, horny, hunter, Milf. Addicted to my lust, and always game for another play.

Sands of time, shifting in the wind. Summer would be hot and heavy. The young Korean men were scheduled and chosen for being different and special. We waited with utmost impatience for those meetings.

A year of longing. Sexy vids and pics to feed those needs — theirs and mine. Vid sex explosions. Touching flesh and blood would never be the same, and this one-time love, the best blow and sex, would be the sweetest memory to last a lifetime.

CHAPTER SIX

D-DAY

DIZZYLAND

"Are you ready for Dizzyland?"

Yes. My dream was coming true. Going to Seoul was something I'd been wanting to do before Covid started, and ever since I saw my first Kdrama, I was hooked.

I used to ridicule people who watched Kdrama. Sad stories, lots of crying, too much drama. Winter Sonata was popular then, and I was young and obsessed with anything Japanese. How could Korean entertainment be better than Japanese? Anime came from Japan, and their Japanese miniature gardens touched my heart like no other.

And then I started watching Kdrama and the Kwave caught me as it had done with millions of people across the globe. The tropes were age-old, from the days of Cinderella and Joseon kings and princesses, written with an Asian blend. Instead of the white prince, this new breed of rich, pretty boys with chocolate abs was catching on.

The Asian male specimen was no longer seen as weak and effeminate. With the rise of Kpop, Kdrama, and Kbeauty, Korean men wore a men's line of skincare, with taut muscles, gentlemanly behaviors, and melodious voices that melted hearts.

It was every woman's dream to have that romantic, rich, smart guy who only had eyes for the cute, smart, and above-average pretty girl who had the bravery and persistence to struggle through life hardships, and to be rewarded with a perfect family and wealth, love and happiness.

It wasn't just this trope; the mystery thrillers, lawyer politics, and sci-fi, fantasy adventures were well-written, too. So, yes, I was hooked for a while, and when the time came for me to reach out and interact with this new species of men across the Pacific in the country called South Korea, I had to take that plunge. Ometv made it possible, and there was no turning back.

It had been about six months since I made first contact with the Korean guys from Ometv and dating apps like Tinder and Bumble. We met off the app on Insta and Kakao and became fast friends and online lovers. Some I'd spoken to every other day, and others we were eager to share our naughty pics and vids, and couldn't wait to meet in real life.

After spending weeks arranging meetings and making a list of the top guys I wanted to meet, it was time to go.

"Excited?" H asked.

A grin popped from my cheeks. Any mention of Seoul or Dizzyland — rainbows and sunshine lit my head. A halo of happy thoughts and fun to come blurred my everyday existence.

The plane landed at Incheon Airport and taxied to the runway. My heart was thumping to the drums in my head. My phone was instantly turned on, and already I'd sent messages to my Korean guys that I was here. All who were between the ages of 25-33 years, hot and cute in their own ways, and working in different professions, were the everyday Korean guy.

Many replied in a snap. I wasn't the only one counting the days. It had been months, and each Byeontae guy had plans to play with their favorite Milf.

It was my first Summer in Seoul, and I felt like it was going to be the best summer ever. Despite being with my family — mom, husband, and kids, nothing was going to destroy the happy bubbles in my head.

It was late afternoon when we reached our hotel in Myeongdong. Already, I had seen some cuties at the airport and was beaming from the rush of entering my Dizzyland.

We dropped by to see my mom in her country. I was counting those days while we got over our jet lag before flying together to Seoul. The plans were that daytime was family vacation time, and night was for the cougar to run free in the city.

"Three rooms?" The hotel receptionist asked. "Passports, please?"

Whoa, I forgot about this. Each room needed an identity. I got a hotel room for my play because I wanted to be close to my family and not wander in the city alone. We were new, and I should call the shots.

The playroom. Yes, I'd leveled up. A separate bag packed with lingerie, toys, cuffs, gels, and oils. Extra Victoria S panties are ready to be soiled for the lucky few.

I gave my mom's passport for the third room, even though she was sleeping with the kids.

"Please have the room on a different floor," I told the front desk.

"You don't want your mother with you?" Front desk guy looked confused.

I shook my head hard. "No. No. Further the better." Thoughts bursting through my mind of naked bodies wrapping over each other, sounds of ecstasy, and the slapping of flesh against flesh.

A blush crept up my face.

This was my first — booking a hotel room for sex. Aside

from the adulteress cherry-picking, I'd not met anyone after. I was beyond nervous.

South Korea was my playground.

I wore a red lingerie. Half-laced cups hugging my breasts and a silky skirt that hung flirty above my knees. Over it, I wore a simple black dress.

"Where do we meet?" YS messaged.

"At the lobby elevator?" I said.

"Okay."

The elevator door opened, and I stepped out. Looked around and hid behind the pillars close by as the music from the hotel bar played some smooth jazz.

"I'm almost here," he said. He was taking a taxi.

I glanced at the large front sliding doors flanked by some animal sculptures. My heart is hammering in my chest. I tried to remember what he looked like, reminding me of the days of blind dates from long ago, before I met H.

YS appeared in a white coat. Taller and broader-shouldered than what I envisioned and a lot cuter than the vid calls we had.

"Hey," he said. His English had a touch of an accent. He resorted to Korean because he felt most comfortable speaking.

"Wanna get a beer?" he asked, and I nodded and followed him out of the hotel to a convenience store a few steps across the street.

It was my first Korean convenience store. A corner shop, tight with health stuff, shavers, soap, personal nick-nacks, snacks, drinks, ramyeon, and microwavable foods.

He got two cans of Kloud beer for himself and me, and we walked casually back to my hotel and up to my room.

"This is my first time doing this," I mumbled.

YS nodded. "I don't come to hotels."

"How do you meet girls?" I asked him. He was a casual playa. Not the rude, arrogant type, but with his looks, he could get anyone he wanted, except that in his dating profile, he liked mature women. Milfs were his all-time fav, and curves got him high. When he matched me, he was beyond excited. DM-ing me every day for new pics and vids and sharing his sex tapes.

"Go to their place? Or they come to mine," he said. "I live close to here. About ten minutes by bus." He gestured out the hotel window.

"Oh…" I said. Actually, I knew that. In fact, it was one of the reasons I picked that hotel because it was close.

We small-talked as we drank. Then, he chugged the rest of his can and dropped his phone. I backed away and dropped onto the bed.

He fell onto me. Lips crushed against mine and kissed me hard.

Hands landed straight on my breasts, massaging them expertly. "I wanted to do this for a long time," he said. "Finally."

And he was right. Finally.

We kissed like rabid rabbits. Stripping our clothes in a flash. He stopped and admired my red lingerie before pulling down the top to reveal my succulent globes of flesh. Taking each in his mouth, he sucked hard as his hand dropped expertly between my legs.

YS was cute, and his body was skin-tight with smooth abs, broad-shouldered, and melting hot. His radio voice was smooth and low as he moaned. Each of his thrusts was deep, and he drilled into my core.

We doggy and he flipped me over and missioned. Pulling a pillow under my waist, trapping my hips against his.

He cummed, and we rested as he watched me play with my dildo and splashed all over him. We washed up, and he had to go, but he stayed. We had another round of sex and then hugged and chatted. He washed, and as I was about to go next to clean up, he dragged me back into bed and maniacally thrust in me again.

"I have to go. Have to work early tomorrow," he panted. It was past two a.m.

Blushing with orgasm, I stared straight into his beautiful Asian eyes. Almond-shaped and coffee brown. His handsome face was also flushed.

"Can we meet again?" I asked.

He checked his phone. "Maybe."

I nodded. I wasn't planning for the second round. My time was scarce, and I had six planned. If I met him again, I'd have to make some changes.

He kissed me hard. His tongue wrapped around mine. Hot breaths in my ear as he sucked and licked me down my throat, to my breast, and latched onto my nipple.

He sighed. "I have to go."

"You can film the next time," I said.

He nodded and smiled. Perv to perv. I knew how to get him.

My mind was whirling as fumes of lust meandered through my thoughts. Not bad, Dizzyland. Kdrama no lie. Hot Asian guys do exist.

My first mouse.

First day. First night. First sex.

Let the marathon begin.

SMELL THE ROSES

I t was his fantasy, Outdoors with his hand between my legs.

We talked to death about it, planning what naughty, sexy things we'd do when we meet. It was many months before we'd meet in the Summer in Seoul. When heat was still in our loins, and we were attracted even though we met online and vid sex was the only high we could get, that was enough.

"Do you think we'll still be talking by then? Isn't it a long time to wait?" I asked.

"I can wait. I'm good at waiting," he said.

HY wasn't really my type. Age-wise and looks, he wasn't Kboy cute and hot. He was also sly because, like many guys online, they catfished and he'd uploaded his pics ten years ago when he was still in college and super cute and mischievous then.

It didn't take much digging to know he wasn't how he looked before, especially after he'd shown his Kakao, and I saw his present pics.

"Hey, those pics in your dating profile are old," I said. I have a thing about being tricked by really old pics. Trust is important to me.

"Oh…hahhaha. I don't take many pics," he said.

"Right…you chose your best ones," I added an emoticon of an annoyed face.

I was onto him. These Koreans like to fake it as far as they can. I don't get it. The ruse would be pulled off the moment we meet.

Catfishing. It seemed very prevalent amongst the Koreans, whose image meant everything to them. Maybe they think that through some chatting, the personality wouldn't matter anymore? Not saying others don't. Maybe my pool was skewed.

I get that. Online gaming and hiding behind the screen made it possible. And with AI, no one would ever know what you really look like. And if you don't like the way you look, with money, you can carve yourself a new face.

I'm old school. It is tempting to have a new nose, but the thought of going under for that, what if I don't wake? I have too much to lose. I plan to live a long, long life.

"No surgery," my family said.

I'm thankful that I'm loved the way I am. However, losing a few pounds wouldn't hurt my esteem. In fact, losing those thirty pounds was the reason why my fans went nuts because those curves took on a whole new sexy.

Hourglass. Yes, my pride. Women got curves, and if we got them, we should flaunt them. Shame on those naysayers who said thin is good and curves are not.

We all have our types. So, girl, don't you think that hot young Korean/Asian guy won't like you? You never know his type till you try. Do-ja giving up now, girl?

"I like thick women. The bigger the breasts and the bigger the ass, the better," said HY, my new friend.

"I've a mummy tummy," I said, embarrassed that he wanted to see all of me, and to take my hands off the parts that embarrassed me.

"I love all of it. Every curve is beautiful," he said.

And yes, Koreans are great at their sweet words, and love

bombing is insane there, but my ears loved to hear what my heart did.

My husband saying how my body is beautiful wasn't the same. After being with someone for two decades, you lose your sense of perspective. It's hard not to think your loved ones are biased because beauty was the eye of the beholder.

HY's words meant something. And those fans and friends made all the difference.

Age was just a number, and though HY was ten years younger than I, rather than the twenty-year gap that I preferred, he was a true friend. Sex wasn't the only thing we talked about. And he was someone who respected my time and my moods.

"I'm happy with myself. At this point in my life, I don't care what people think," he smiled. "I'm not tall, but I have a big one," he laughed as we headed to his car.

We were going to lunch and met for the first time in the hotel lobby by the elevator, where I met every guy. A famous pork chop store at Namsan and a drive around Myeongdong so he could show me some parts of the city.

I was wearing a one-piece Christmas-green dress. Sleeveless and hugged my body like snake-skin, skimming my knees, and slipping up my thighs when I sat. A pair of white sneakers and my LV bag to add to the Fit.

If someone were to see us together, we could look like a married couple, because he looked thirty-five and I looked like the mid-30s, or maybe younger. He was an ajusshi, and I was one who refused to face reality.

"People are looking...," I said, hiding my face with my hand as we strolled along the castle walls with cute cafes lining our other side.

"I wish I wore something more normal," I said. "Maybe, black, white, or more conservative." My boobs and curves look too big in the crowd. For a few minutes, I was back to my old shy self.

"You look beautiful and sexy," HY smiled. "Don't worry about what people think."

He was right. Confidence was everything. Who the fuck cared? The Milf cougar prowled the day. No more lurking in the night. Seoul men, beware, and girls take note, the big cat was hunting today.

We got into his car, and as he drove around the city, his hand reached for my thigh. Bright afternoon sun lit our smiling faces, and as we waited by a bus on his left side, his fingers crept up under my dress.

The traffic light was red, and cars pulled up around us. Music blasting in his normal sedan.

"Do you want it?" I asked him, giggling. We were being crazy.

Why shouldn't we do what we want? This was his country, and if he was fine, I should be too.

My right hand went under my dress and hooked my black laced T-panty. Like a fisherman, I pulled the panties down and out as he watched and laughed.

Like a stripper, I twirled my panties with my finger and tossed them at him.

"For me?" he grinned.

"Yes," I giggled.

He kept my panties and then dropped his hand to my smooth skin. His car skimmed across the lanes as his hand rubbed my thigh, inching in each time when he could drive with one hand. At the same time, my hands reached for his raw stick. Lips brushing his sensitive skin when I could.

We laughed, moaned, and played, not caring if the world saw. The sun smirked as his car dove deep into the parking garage. We were back in my hotel.

He parked between two cars, and I turned to him. "What about the CCTVs? And the black boxes?" I pointed to the cars beside us.

"They can't see us," he said.

His hands pulled down the top of my dress, and my boobs sprang out. The bra was already gone during our daring drive through Seoul.

Mouth nursing my large nipples as his hands went between my thighs. He pushed me between the front seats. Stuck between the sides, he grabbed my hips and thrusted.

I gasped loudly and cried as he hammered hard. Hand over my mouth, he kept pounding. The sounds of cars screeching through the garage levels didn't stop him.

Over and over, he thrusted into me. His hot breath behind my ear, his hands pulling my wavy hair back like a stallion humping his rider.

"I'm cumming," I moaned. "I'm cumming."

"Me too…you," he groaned, and then a car appeared.

FEED ME FETISH

What is your fetish?

That's the second question I'd usually ask in my Byeontae Game. The first was when he had his first sex. The way the game worked was I asked the question, and he responded, and then I shared my answer too for that question, and the same with his questions.

Most guys would say their first sex was with someone they met or knew. Their first was in ranges, either really young, like 12-15 years, or older, like when they were from 17-23 years old. There were a few who were still cherry virgins at 25 years old.

"If a guy is still a virgin at around 23 and up, he's a loser," someone said.

Yes, I deserved better. I didn't have to settle for virgins. But, sometimes, my lusty greed wins the battle.

People are people. Everyone had their own path, insecurities, and reasons for things.

The 'Cherries' had their stories, but as I'd told the many young guys, I was there to play and not teach them life lessons on sex. And though I was a cougar, 'popping cherry boys' was not my kink.

Kink vs. Fetish, what's the diff?

Not much, frankly. Fetish is the moment you can get super horny when something was done, or something you saw triggered it. And no, seeing a naked woman with big boobs while eating juicy wings doesn't count.

Kink is an action that you pursue, going for it with passion because that's what you love. This could be specific BDSM acts like Shibari, or maybe Milfs in hot, rich mommy clothes vs. pounding a Milf talking to her husband on the phone, which was more of a fetish.

The lines are blurred.

And as for Byeontae? A pervert is always seeking his/her fetish and kink. Or creating new ones because the mind won't stop thinking of sexy fun. Like food porn. Always wanted to try that. And no, not the James Bond-y type of naked Asian women on the table with sushi on them. Sides, raw fish and sex stinks.

In my journey, I'd come across different fetishes and kinks. My questions opened the floodgates, and I got to hear these guys' secret confessions on what they really like. I won't bother you with normal stuff, and even some listed here were normalized these days. Here are some I learned:

Feet and shoes (stepping on bodies, jerking off with feet, sex with heels on) — the guys say pretty feet were nice shapes and arches.

I'd say I don't know the diff. I don't have an intensity for feet, but there is one act I enjoyed with a man's toes, but I won't say here. Only the very lucky guys get to experience it.

Socks, tights, leggings, body stockings — tearing them off gives the guy and girl the feeling of control or lack of. I personally like this. Bondage is one of my favorite plays.

Collecting torn-up stockings is a kink. Insisting that all women you have sex with need to wear a pair of new stockings, that is a fetish.

Spit — spitting fish back and forth in mouths, dirty blowjobs, spitting in pussies, in ears, anywhere with holes. Frankly, why don't you just use cum, you might ask. I agree. But we all must be safe, careful adults, and people who spit might not like cum, which brings me to another story about cum. There are double standards to it. Guys who want women to swallow but won't kiss their lips after. Dude…come on…

Vomit — yes, it gets grosser. This I'd only heard once among the hundreds of guys I'd spoken to, and to this person. I had to delete, block, and never speak to again.

Engineer J was a twenty-three-year-old civil engineer in another city. He was a replacement guy I met on Bumble whom I spoke to during my first Summer trip in Seoul. My previous guy friend got sick with COVID and cancelled at the last minute. I didn't want to waste that spot, and even though I didn't like to meet strangers and have sex with them until I knew them, I felt this guy was nice and sweet enough for me to eat.

He took the train to see me. About thirty minutes away from Seoul. Nice face, tall, slim, and gentle manner from the video chats we had, and wasn't a catfish. Except, when he came to my hotel room, he said it was his first time meeting in a hotel, and he was a Cherry.

He lied. Well, technically, I didn't ask. We spoke dirty and had some fun on vid chat before I said yes to him coming over. I was in a tight pale green dress and had my green laced bodysuit underneath. My period had just arrived, and I wore a tampon so we could play before we did — tteokbokki.

You might judge how desperate I was to have sex during a period. I'd say I was just min-maxing my stay in Seoul. At that time, I wasn't sure I was coming back to Korea, and I didn't want to waste my chance to eat as many Korean meals as I could. It was my first stint at a sex marathon, and in the end, I knocked out five different guys out of the park.

Did I get over my Korean men addiction after my first summer? Obviously not. Because I went back again the next summer, and that experience was different from the first.

Back to Engineer J. Yes, Cherry boy.

"Why haven't you had sex yet?" I asked. "Didn't you say you had a girlfriend?"

"I did. But we didn't have sexual intercourse," he said. His English was good. There was no 'lost in translation' with him.

His lips were on mine. His hands were grabbing my dress and pulling it over my head. In fact, it got stuck halfway, and he was squeezing my breasts and sucking my nipples when I finally got the dress off.

He kept saying how beautiful and sexy I was. He was a tall, skinny guy, but he loved women with curves. My hourglass figure and large ass were his favorite parts, and his long fingers held my butt like holding treasure.

"Can I take pics?" He asked.

"Yes," I replied, my heart swayed by his words, and filming and pics were my fetish.

I posed for him, and he spanked my ass hard and well as he filmed — it was his first time spanking, but he had some natural skill to the art of spanking.

"How can you be a virgin?" I asked him after he spanked and made me crawl on the floor, and dry humped me as he fingered me and made me cum.

He was in my mouth. He used my dildo in me, and knew what he was doing.

"I can't stay hard in a pussy. I've only cummed in the mouth. I thought if I did it with a hot Milf like you, I could," he said.

This was his fear.

And he proved it true when we tried. He went limp. We moved to the window, and he stuck his shaft in my mouth. Pumping hard, making popping sounds. He groaned, "I'm coming...I'm coming..." He overflowed everywhere — all over my chest and dripped to the ground.

"I didn't masturbate for a month," he confessed.

"Why?" I asked as I cleaned up. Overall, the experience was low mid. But I chose to meet. At least, I got some nice pics and vids from it.

"Have you heard of a man's Chi?" He asked.

"A little?" I said, reminded of Busan Guy, L, who told me about his problems — he had a big kink for Milfs, and couldn't have sex with girls his age and cum.

"I have a sex problem because I started porn too early. I was ten. I watched and jerked off too much for many years, and so I'm desensitized," Engineer J said. "I can't get hard watching normal porn. I have to keep watching something crazier."

"Like what?" I asked.

"I'm not a disgusting pervert. I'm a nice guy...," he said. "Also, I've been trying not to masturbate for a longer time because my Chi is precious. A man's seed is a life force. If I cum too much, I lose my Chi."

The man's Chi. Another topic of discussion. A survey I'd take later.

"And so?" I sensed he was holding in.

We were sitting on a loveseat, side by side. I was in my wine-red satin robe, and he was in his white T-shirt and grey underwear. It wasn't what I imagined as sexy, but I felt the playtime session was over.

It was therapy time.

"Don't tell me you are into poop," I said.

"No! No! But, I like golden shower..." He glanced at me and smiled.

"Okay...I've heard of that. Not done it, but if it was done in the bathroom and on my leg, I might be okay to try," I said, and he smiled.

Within reason, I'm fine. I was trying to be open-minded.

"What about..." He continued talking and asking questions and gauging what I was comfortable with, until it got to here.

"Vomit," he said.

"Vomit?" My brows crinkled. Frankly, just saying that word made me sick.

"Yeah. There is this Asian girl. She has a channel. She pukes and masturbates." He showed me the video.

"Wtf..." I stood up. "Dude, that's too much. Is that your kink?"

Okay, there was a limit to non-judging. I told him no blood, no murder, no mutilation. If the guy likes those, I didn't have to be part of it.

"I don't know why." He stared at his hands.

And stupid me asked to see it, and even more, told H about it after.

"Block, delete, get rid of him."

And so I did. Engineer J was out of life with a few taps. I didn't want to ghost or block if I really didn't have to. It went both ways;

we deserved closure, but even though I didn't clearly say it to him, Engineer J should know why.

Fetishes and Kinks. As said, people are different and have different needs, but there are lines we don't cross.

Where was the vomit? So, another guy liked burping. Women who burp on command and during sex. Maybe there are those who like women crying. If spanking, whipping, and BDSM cuffs, plugs, mouth balls, and nipple clamping were okay, what else is okay?

Nothing seems far-fetched in the minds of people, and what sexually triggers them.

To burp or to puke, that was the question.

Well, mine was simple. "Don't puke where you eat."

—oo—

CHICK MAGNET

—oo—

I ate at KFC that night.

Not the chicken but the humankind. It would have been great if it came with a mug of beer. Always wanted to try ChiMek, which I only saw in dramas. The way those people savor the crunchiness of the chicken as they take their bite into that juicy, finger-licking drumstick, followed by the fizzling, slightly sweet sensation of foamy beer as it flows down their throats.

Yes. I want it too. The hot and cold. The cute and hunky Korean man that the Korean media so easily flaunts. As H called it — the Korean machine.

K-pop stars and Korean actors are plastered online and on airwaves with their perfect, tight, smooth bodies and 6-pack abs. Babyface boys grinning with dirty minds as they used you and dropped you when the next girl came along.

Wasn't asking much. Just a night with one of these delectable young, hot guys. A score to settle, just like they had one too.

Who doesn't love a Milf? Apparently, every guy does. It was on their bucket list just as mine was. Finding the right fit is always a challenge. I was sick of vanilla sex, and with each I met, I leveled up.

I got my own KFC for a one-nighter, on that last day of my Yolo-ing alone in my hotel room away from my family. It was the second summer in Seoul, and unlike the first, I was given three days away from my family in a different hotel across the Hangang River.

Yes, I was coddled. So, that weekend, I was brought to my senses. Reality wasn't what I'd pictured, and for a foodie, life was harsh when you are left waiting for guys who broke promises to take you out for yummy Korean meals, and then play.

So, it started like this. With peanuts.

"I want to go back," I sobbed on the phone.

"You can't come back. You asked for this time away," said H. He was talking about how I'd told my family that I was on a business trip and moved to the other side of Gangnam River to a hotel of my own so I could meet my friends. But things didn't turn out as planned and I was almost kidnapped by a Korean Catfisher, and guys were bailing.

"I haven't eaten anything proper in the past days," I said. This was too much for a foodie like me. Each meal was supposed to be savored.

"What happened to your dates?" H asked.

"Only my Fwb kept the appointment. The Katsu at Namsan Tower was yummy. The rest of the guys kept canceling – sick, work, drunk..."

"What did you eat for lunch and dinner?" I asked. He was giving me the details on the delectable foods my children and him had and my stomach was growling in frustration.

This couldn't be the special time I was hoping for. Sex was the purpose, but food was just as important, especially with all the saves I made on Insta months before. I wanted to eat well — the food and humankind.

But the fact that none of those guys were willing to spend time to break bread showed where I stood, or lay.

This sucked. I felt like a freaking whore.

Because of those flakes, I took a chance with a stranger. It was a gamble. One night stands wasn't my thing. The health risks and not knowing that person was risky. Looking back, I won't do that again. But that was my last free day, I wanted to make memories.

"I ate peanuts," I said.

"What?" H laughed.

"Peanuts were my dinner tonight," I replied.

"Go out and grab some food," H said.

"It's not that easy," I said. It was all excuses. I knew if I walked far enough and searched Google or Naver, I'd find something my gourmet tummy would like. If I were serious about filling up my tummy, I could eat anything.

But, I was in pity mode. Pitying my current state of things, and as I said before, I was coddled. I blamed the terrible traffic, where everything seemed so far away. Just to meet someone, it took at least forty minutes to an hour.

"Peanuts," I said to myself. "What would you do if you only ate peanuts?" I said to the wall, and to my phone as I swiped for the next stranger guy to meet.

My eyes riveted onto the pics in his profile. "No freaking way." Why would a guy like him be on a dating app? He should have girls lining up just to meet him. I was checking his page for catfishing. The photographs looked real enough. He wasn't crazy, amazingly handsome like Cha Eun Woo, but he could pass as one of those Kpop B-listers or a supporting role in a Kdrama. Enough to cause many heads to turn.

"Hi :)" I sent him a text on Bumble. A chat replied in a snap.

"Hello," he replied. "Are you in Seoul?"

Typical for a one-nighter to ask. "Yes," I replied.

"Where are you?" he asked.

"Myeongdong," I said.

"Good. I'm at work now. It's about twenty minutes from my office."

"Oh. That's not far…" I replied.

"Do you want to meet?" he asked. My heart was beating fast. No way. Is this for real?

"Do you like older women?" I asked. I checked his profile. He was twenty-seven.

"Yes. Very much. Do you like young guys?"

"I do." I smiled to myself.

"Where do you want to meet?" he asked. "Have you eaten?"

He was one of the few to ask me that. Already earning brownie points for being polite.

"Not yet," I said.

"Okay, we can meet in Myeongdong Street and maybe pick up food there. I haven't eaten too," he said.

It was almost 8:30 pm. I glanced at my bottle of peanuts and grinned. Can't let this fish swim away.

"Let's meet first at a Sulbing and decide," I said. Sulbing was a shaved ice franchise. Summer was tourist season, and the place was jam-packed with Asian tourists.

I got there first and was giggling to myself. I imagine him weaving through the gaggles of gossipy ajummas (old aunts) and ajooshis (old uncles) to get to me. True enough, when he arrived, he looked horrified when all the tourists turned their heads at once, like some zombie movie, eyeing him. They were probably wondering what this handsome, young Korean guy was doing in their realm of ice-cold dessert feasting.

It was worth a laugh when he caught my gaze, and I went to him, not wanting the poor guy to beg any further.

"Do you want coffee or tea?" He asked, glancing at me after we got out of Sulbing, finally away from the crowds. Coffee wasn't the choice of drink on a Sunday night. Most office people were probably at home resting before the start of a new week.

"I'm hungry…" I glanced at him again, and he caught my gaze.

A group of young girls was heading for us and whispering when they saw him by my side. He preened, and the girls smiled, all ignoring the Milfy beside him. I wondered if they thought I was a relative. Most, I assumed, wouldn't think I was going to lay him tonight. Our age gap was big, and though I looked young, I was still a young aunt in age.

We decided to head back to my room and order delivery. In the elevator on the way up, two white girls kept glancing back at us, faces filled with envy. Each had a BTS keychain on their bag and was whispering in a European language.

Even if we didn't sleep that night, it'd be worth peanuts. Having an arm candy was my first, and who didn't love being envied?

We stepped into my room. He grabbed me from behind, arms circling my waist. "I want you." He whispered into my ear. Being a head taller than me, he bent and kissed my neck as I turned around. The dark dress I wore hid a surprise.

"I love the color bright red. Like the color of painted nails," he texted earlier. "Do you paint your nails?"

It was too late to find some nail polish, but I wanted to give him something he could fantasized about. A night with them was a night to be remembered.

"It's bright red." His jaw dropped when I pulled off my dress.

It was my Wonder Woman suit — bright red, plastic smooth corset. My breasts are bolstered by padding, adding to my already large breasts. With my golden roped stockings and red whip, it'd be steps from the goddess.

But I wasn't sure if he was into cosplay, and I didn't want to scare my one-nighter away.

"Wow…" his eyes riveted to my breasts. He was definitely Team Boob because his hands slapped onto my twin appendages and trailed up and down my smooth boob shield.

"It's beautiful," he said.

It didn't take long to shed his clothes and to remove my red armor for his lips to latch on to my perky nipples. He sucked them like a babe to a mom. Massaging my breasts like clay mounds, moaning and groaning as he pounded me hard.

His long legs trapped mine in between as he lay on me, pushing me to the ground and then pulling out my arms till my face rubbed the carpet. His pounding on the carpet bruised my cheeks. I cried, moaning and grunting as he pushed in deeper and out and in again and again. He never let off, until I cummed and till he did.

We stopped for our fried chicken and chatted as he told me what he did for work and what he loved the most, which was a J-pop artist whom he surprisingly looked almost identical to.

I asked if we could film, and he helped me with my lace mask. My phone turned on with flash as he filmed my mouth taking him whole. The sounds of his growl could be heard through the sloppy blow job I gave him, sensually massaging his penis with my tongue and mouth.

He pushed my head down and deep-throated me as he cummed. We had sex more times, all breasts and assess pounding, making enough film to please the eyes of my fans who loved reading my stories and watching my dirty films.

We showered and went to bed. It was weird, and it was my second time having a sleepover; the first was with Busan Guy the Summer before, and I didn't know what to do.

Perhaps it was an unspoken rule to sleepovers in a one-nighter, I didn't know. Was it a Korean habit? With language barriers and a guy who kept talking about his J-pop idol, we were lost in translation. And when he fell asleep, and I was still awake, I wondered what the hell I was doing.

I wasn't going to sleep that night. Not because I wanted more but because a stranger was in my bed. A guy I met two hours ago and two hours before chatted online in a country that wasn't my own.

In the wee hours of the morning, I felt an arm over my shoulder. A scent I was unfamiliar with and a body, not my husband's.

Have I gone too far? Stubbornly wanting to prove that I was Yolo-ing, and my tears shed weren't fails.

His lips were on my nipple, and his head was nestling on my boob. He needed a mommy, not a lover. Despite how hot he might be, this wasn't what I wanted.

"Didn't you have morning sex?" Someone asked after.

"No," I replied.

"What? Isn't he super hot."

"Yeah. But hot boys can be babies, and men are boys," I said.

"True." That someone laughed.

"This cougar needs to be fed, and my hunt is still on."

"So how was the fried chicken?" H asked.

"Better than peanuts," I said.

MILFY BY DAY

Someone always ends up on the floor.

Knees down, and maybe a good time crawling. One thing I learned from the two years of Yolo-ing is that the best sex is a play of passion and power.

Assert or be taken.

There is no right or wrong. Whatever gets you high, your kinks and fetishes, is all good. This is the one time you can release the ropes binding you and be free, or you could have strings attached if that's your thing.

"Meeting a Milf has always been my dream." The nice ones would say that. What they really want to do is fuck that older woman and check that box.

There are two types of guys — the subs and the doms.

The submissive wanted to be led and eaten.

"I eat young men for breakfast," I'd tell them. That always got them excited. Their imaginations running wild — my slippery mouth on their hardness, sucking and licking with my puppy tongue. Running my fingers up and down their shafts, and then grabbing their balls with my hands and squeezing, as their lips puckered up, low groans escaping their throats.

I am a cougar and a Milf. A deadly sexy combo, adding Asian to it. I'm their dreams come true, Japanese porn alive. Big boobs and ass, an hourglass meant to be grabbed.

Many have never heard of the term — cougar. Neither did I when I first started. Milf, on the other hand, everyone knew.

The first time I heard that Milf was in American Pie, when Finch slept with Stifler's mom. It was a dumb, sexy movie that resonated with all of us growing up in that era, and though she wasn't a looker, there was something really naughty and exciting about it.

Sometimes, I slip up, revealing our differences generations apart. I try not to because I didn't want to be reminded of the years, preferring to match minds and bodies rather than what society expects.

Initially, when I started dating, my age range was 25-35 years. Hanging out with moms who are thirty-five made me realize I was no different and perhaps even younger in thinking. I got along well with my kids, sharing in their media and way of thought. Because I like reading, social media, and music, I belonged to a generation that was not my own. Adding to the Asian fountain of youth, I could pass off as being in my early thirties.

Ageism is bull crap.

We live in a world where stereotypes need to be abolished. High-speed Wi-Fi and smartphone screens tore down the walls of society, countries, and traditions. Indeed, the old ways are breaking. Thanks to the Internet and social media, the young are now growing older, and the rest of us and our lives before are swept under the rug. It is hard to imagine there was a time when cell phones didn't exist.

"I don't know why or when I started liking older, mature women," L said. He was twenty-three when I first met him on Bumble. A Korean guy from Busan. His English wasn't the best, but good enough for sex talks and translators.

His pics were super hot-cute, and his profile was different because it targeted older women. It was a bait I couldn't resist. At that time, I was also chatting with a twenty-three-year-old vet student on Hinge. He, too, was also into Milfs, and loved my sexy stories.

The thrill of chatting with them was irresistible. In another time or place, our circles wouldn't have connected. The chances of us ever meeting were close to zero, but at this time, with dating apps, social norms meant nothing.

It was true. They were below my acceptable range. Anything over a twenty-year difference should be too much. They were puppies in the world; their lives were barely starting. However, my curiosity about their lives, dreams, and aspirations excited me.

"It is my fantasy to have a Fwb with a Milf. I want to be friends with you forever," L said. "I want to know all about you and find something we have in common."

"When did you start liking Milfs?" I asked. A survey was in the works, and I was collecting data.

"Don't know...maybe eighteen, nineteen? One day I like older women," he said.

"Did you watch a lot of Milf porn?" I asked.

"After I became crazy for Milf, I watched a lot...," he said, "I have many girlfriends. Changing every year, but none of the sex is good. I cannot get hard."

"Why?" I said.

"I went to see a doctor, and he gave me medicine."

"What medicine?"

"I touched myself six times a day. I cannot have sex with young girls. Only older women like you, it is easy to become hard."

"Okay...so what did the doctor say?"

"He said I need to control and not touch. He gave me medicine."

It sounded serious.

L was too young a guy to be suffering from erectile dysfunction. At twenty-three, he should be fucking anything that moved. Strange enough, he wasn't the only one suffering; another guy, a 24-year-old cherry boy, told me a similar story.

Porn addiction.

Was it a problem? Did it cause sexual issues?

"If I were a boy, I'd be playing with my stick every day," I told H. "Imagine a toy you can hold with your hand anytime you want."

H, who was sitting on the bed with his iPad as always, shook his head. "Only you would think like that."

"Yeah. I guess having an erection all the time can be painful…" I pondered. "But I bet when I'm a kid, I'd be putting it in any hole I see."

Yes. Curiosity kills the pussy cat. I got in trouble with the many things I'd put my hands on and poked my nose into something I shouldn't have. It was something innate in all of us that couldn't be helped.

Holes. Glory holes. Another thing my pervert mind loved. A story that I'd tell later because I digress.

L loved stockings. He also loved my vast collection of lingerie and toys, especially leashes. During those three months before we went to Korea, we discussed our plans, and he texted me daily.

"What are you wearing today?" he often asked. He was a barista and worked in shifts. He was also studying the art of coffee making and the beans and aromas. I assumed it was similar to learning about winemaking.

Coffee and cafes were big businesses in Korea and East Asia, and cafe hopping, Instagram, and dating spots were weekend hangouts.

I liked guys who worked hard. Hearing them pursue their work and passions was a sexy plus. As someone said, "The brain is the new sexy." And women, being more sapiens, loved a good brain.

"I want to do it on the bench with you, or somewhere people cannot see, or near people walking. I want you to wear a long coat on an outfit and put two dildos in your vagina and anal."

"Omg. Using a small vibrator with an app?" I asked.

"When the guys are nearby you, I want to turn the dildo with a remote control," he said.

"What if the guys see and become horny?" I asked.

"Or make you masturbate hard at guys' toilet" he said.

"In the toilet stall, when I'm moaning and cumming, and they are hearing. They can see our legs and hear the sounds of you hammering me," I said.

"Really wanna make you mine more and more. Really want to molest you in the train. After you make squirting on the floor. Or try a vibrator and make the chair's seat wet."

The words were addicting, and I grew wet. The temptation of a messed-up pervert's mind was hard to resist.

"I think my head will be full of you during work," he said.

These were badges of honor, words of each guy who couldn't stop thinking of ways to play, to ravage me, and me, the Milf cougar who could please them till their minds grew blank.

I wanted that, too. The dumbness of sex. Where nature took over, and the human receded.

We will mate like animals. We wanted to shout, scream, and be ultimately free.

"Maybe I think I can cumming three times continuously," he said. "Really want to rub my face on your boobs and panties. And want to feel your panty getting wet and lick it. Wanna kiss you and lick, sucking all night long."

"I want to feel your hand on my back, spine down and up my ass, and in between my legs," I said.

"I want to start in the elevator with deep kissing," he said. "And my one arm will hug your waist, and the other will hold your ass. Jesus, now I'm hard when I take your message."

"U can own me for one night," I said.

"Want to make you forget your H," he said.

"You can dress me and take my clothes off. Tie me up. Rub oil, gel, on your body on mine. I will bring my beautiful lingerie," I said.

"Make you creampie until you get pregnant. Fill your holes with mine."

"Please be gentle with me," I said.

"Oh. Yeah sure. Just licking will be first. If you feel really hurt and want to stop… we need a rule for the stopping word…"

"Safe word. Yes. We need one," I said.

"If you say that word, I'll stop. But just say stop, I'll keep going and work harder," he said.

"Okay…" I replied. L always enjoyed the vid calls. Though I didn't see much of his face, because he flipped it fast to his cock and wanted to see my body, I thought I knew him well.

Many times we cummed like this. He loved watching me orgasm and especially loved my big ass. Spanking it made him go crazy, pumping hard, and when I heard him moan, I knew I pleased him well.

He wanted to chat with me every day. Always asking what I

was wearing and to take pictures of my outfits. We chatted about other people and the stories I gained. He was envious of H and jealous at times at the vids we filmed, and yet always asking for more so he could jerk himself off.

Heart-melting grins all around. I was new to this, too. Dating and word games. Flirts and one-nighters. I might be a cougar, but I was a baby compared to these guys, who, with the new-gen attitudes, dated more than I did.

Baby cougar had much to learn. Sweet talk like that was cheap. Plus, Koreans were known to be smooth and had lots of promises, dreams, and charms.

The Internet echoed countless painful lessons, ghosted women of the world. Voices of thousands raised in the air — in numbers, ones, and zeros, digitalized stories of these romantic gestures — the truth hurts.

"You are the one I'm looking for. Cute, sexy, and hot. You are making me so hard. I want to know about your personality. If we want to last, I want to know you more than just sex. So I'm worried about you leaving me when you're tired of me," he said. "I like your personality now. I love your smiles."

"I think u will leave me first," I said. They all do. Post-nut clarity. It was inevitable. But at least, we should have a brief fling, a time of fun and cherished memories. This was what I hoped for with all my Fwbs.

"I will always be here," I told some of them. I was the loyal one. The friend who would be there. When the sex ran out, I would be here to listen. The ear of a stranger to calm their anxieties, sadness, and anger when life took them wrong. Or a happiness to share, which I would share in return.

"Hahah, no," he said, "I will stay. I said many times I have a hot, mature woman fetish. You are the dream girl I really imagined."

His words touched me. Because of the months we shared, despite the shards buried in my heart from the many who left without a word of goodbye, I wanted to believe.

A friend who would respect me. Who cherished what I had given and would give back what was offered.

Our plans were made; he would take the day off, and we would go around Busan and have dates, food, and lots of sex.

One day, just a month or so before our scheduled meeting, he disappeared halfway through a conversation.

The more the sugar lips pile, the higher the fall. And I fell for it. Plunging headfirst. Thought I was dead. But I got back up again, dusted my knees, and learned a new lesson learned.

I went to Korea as I planned. Got to see Dizzyland, and played with the mice. A scar was buried in my chest as I glanced at Busan and saw him in every nook and cranny. Tears running down my cheeks.

And on the last day before I was to fly and leave Korea, I got a special message.

It was L. He was back.

—o THOUGHTS: o—

"You gotta have a heart of steel. These people aren't real."

I wished I could follow through with those words. After being ghosted and love-bombed so much, I wished I could say three years of Yolo that I'd be barbed with spikes and nothing could seep into my pulsating heart of gold.

Korean guys, with Kdrama in their blood, were generally nice and kind. Gentlemanly behaviors did exist there. And, despite being typical horny, thirsty guys, their honeyed words got in deep.

At that point in this story, after my first trip, I had my heart and ego broken at least three times.

Tears ran deep, and those guys were experts at promising affection and making plans to meet, tour, and play, only to disappear, block, and make you cease to exist.

A complete package. Sweet and cruel.

I'd been told by other Koreans that ghosting was a way to let the person go. To not end with harsh words and feelings.

I beg to differ. To me, it was the cowardly way out. Maybe I'd become too American and live with confrontation.

I believed in facing a relationship, or friendship, that you felt had ended, with dignity. Pulling off that bandaid when the wound had not healed.

It was the adult thing to do.

To tell how you felt, and that this was over. To not leave someone hanging with what-ifs and what-did-I-do-wrong, or risk a block.

"It is psychologically scarring to leave without a goodbye. It creates insecurity, anger, lower self-esteem, and so on," I said to a Korean friend. I had to talk this out.

Why was a culture the way it was? When did the actions of some people ghosting become a chicken-and-egg event, resulting in a possessive relationship marked by distrust?

At one point, there was happiness. Or was all that friendly, happy chatter and sex a fake?

I guess it could be. Aside from society and culture, men and women treat connections differently. Women didn't have Hyeonja (현자) Time. We didn't have post-nuts.

Of course, not everyone was like that. It'd be like stereotyping a whole race and gender to be a type when humans were all different in degrees.

Perhaps it was my way to cope with the rejections. Coming out Yolo-ing had strengthened my ego, but when the chase ended with my prey escaping, it was disappointing.

The first trip to Seoul was fun. Firsts were always that way, and the five guys I met were mostly what I'd been wishing for.

Others whom I'd not mentioned in my stories — one was a broken guy whom I'd enjoyed watching his mirror cum spraying on vid chat, turned out to be more shy, and who could perform once before leaving quickly.

The other was a director who tattooed his name on his body and proudly proclaimed his dream of becoming famous. He had fingers that hammered like a machine piler.

"Tonight would be a test drive. Like a race car driving a circuit," said the God Director.

God Director was hot and handsome, younger-looking than his age. But his ego probably couldn't take the fact that I didn't call him back for a second round, and when I DM him finally, it was because I saw an advertisement that reminded me of him.

A year later, I met him on Bumble again, as if he had been waiting to catch up with me, after we had promised to meet the following year.

A year later, I "liked" him, but he never responded. I guess, life went on. Some memories were meant to stay that way.

As for L, my twenty-three-year-old young one from Busan. It was a story of myriad temptations, therapy, and confusion.

Fish come, and fish go. The tank leaked, and it was time to mend the hole. My heart might break, but those cracks will patch, and only time will tell if it was really worth the effort.

CHAPTER SEVEN

TEARS FOR FEARS

—oo—

TRAIN FROM BUSAN

—oo—

Serendipity wasn't fated; it was created.

And how much did I want it to happen? Enough to change my flight plans for him. L was one of the reasons I went to Seoul in the first place.

"Boob vs. Butt. Choose. Which one are you?" It was my version of MBTI. "Forget Myers-Briggs," I'd say. "Mine is much easier."

Yes. A four-letter word could tell instantly the type of person you are.

And another four letters could tell this guy had a problem.

"Milf," L said. "I love Milfs, and I didn't leave you. My phone cut off. I cannot log in. Kakao didn't let me. I talked to them many times, and they just gave me back my account yesterday."

"Did you remember I was going to be in Busan?" I asked him.

"Yes. I know. The 17th. But, I cannot contact you."

It was true. L and I weren't smart enough to think it through. We should have exchanged numbers instead of relying on the social app. And even if we did, his phone might have died, and he had to get a new one. And if we really were smarter, we'd exchange emails too, and if that didn't work, our mailing address.

That was too much. For a Fwb, this had the makings of a relationship.

"I thought you dropped me," I told L. I was new to the game then. A few months into Yolo-ing, I met him on Tinder. He was really cute and just my type with his young boyish looks and extremely filthy mind and mouth. My type of byeontae.

"No! I didn't. My Insta didn't work, either, and I forgot your ID."

Thinking back, I wondered if they were lies. It was very convenient that he said the same things many other guys did. Was Insta so bad of an app that guys were kicked out, and when they were finally back, they remembered what my ID was? Could he have started a new account and looked for me earlier rather than waiting months to contact me? My ID was a very easy name to remember as it was in Korean.

"I'm flying tomorrow," I said.

"I know. I'm too late." L added a sad face. "Now, we have to wait until next year to meet."

That was a trigger. L threw the bait.

Yes. I am a firefly. Always worried that my flame would snuff out at any moment and my life would be filled with regrets. Impulsive. And, I was a Team Butt person.

"Your boobs or your butt?" Someone asked. "Show me a pic of your butt, and I'll choose."

"Not my boobs and butt. What do you like? It's a personality test, dude," I replied to that person.

"It's hard to choose…"

I rolled my eyes. I was dealing with another indecisive person. "If you can't choose, you're greedy and indecisive."

"What's that?"

"You can't make a decision," I said.

"Boobs," someone said.

"Boobs means you like comfort, planner, and safety."

"True...I worry it won't be okay. What are you?" Someone asked.

"Butt. Risk taker, impulsive, and passionate."

"Isn't passionate better?" He asked.

"Not really. Many mistakes. Act and think later. Every personality has good and bad," I said.

And in the case of L, he and I were definitely Butt people. "I changed my flight. Pushed it out a day. Can you take time off?" I asked.

"My work ends at 7 pm," he replied.

"I'll get you a KTX ticket," I said. "I don't want to wait a year."

"Me too. I want you...," he said. "Sorry, I can't pay for the ticket."

He was 23 years old. Worked as a barista. "It's okay." This was a cougar talking. Time was more precious than money. For $50, it was better than flying all the way to Seoul and not meeting him.

I'd make fate. "I'll get you the Train from Busan and back."

Our plans were made, and the next day came fast. My heart is hammering in my chest. I went for my first and last chance for a facial, which I'd always wanted to get but didn't because during the Korean trip, I was juggling with naughty meet-ups, touring with my mom and family, and working on my book.

H was long gone to Japan and I had the hotel room to myself. L was the last person I was going to meet in Seoul. A great way to end a first experience in Korea. A memory worth remembering.

As I took the elevator down to meet him in the lobby, I was both excited and nervous. Never had I ever paid for a train ticket to bring a guy to me. Never had I felt more like a mature woman preying on a young man. Adding to our age difference, which would raise eyebrows.

Age was just a number.

"I'm here." The text came after he'd been giving me updates on where he was. My hotel was in Myeongdong where most of the tourists liked to stay. The older part of Seoul is close to the palaces and street markets. A crew of stewardesses flocked in as I got out of the elevator, and I hid, afraid to be caught.

No one knew me. I was in a foreign country, and East Asian, one of the many black-haired women in a mass of many. Guilt reflected in my face as I stared at the mirrored elevator door.

A tall man was approaching me. His face I didn't recognize. His body shape I did. He had nice broad shoulders, long legs, and a V-shaped torso. I knew he was working out and not as slim as he was in his previous pics. Having seen his bottom half more than a couple of times in the months preceding this, and his fashion as he took many to keep me close, I knew he was most likely L.

Still, "Shit," I said to myself. I was catfished again. His face I didn't know. Or did I? He could be L's older brother.

"Hi," he said and reached out to give me a side hug.

I stiffened. Still searching his face for some resemblance. "L?"

"Yeah."

In my heart, I was still reeling. Holy shit. Oh Wtf.

I was new to this. I didn't know what to do. How was I supposed to get out of this? I brought him here. He didn't have a place to stay. How was I supposed to tell him to go home to Busan when he took two and a half hours to travel here to see me?

The questions kept compounding in my head. My eyes were blurry, and my body stiffened more as he sniffed into my hair. It wasn't that he was terrible-looking. It was just upsetting because in my mind, I had expected someone different.

It was a 60:40 chance of being Catfished. 40% was high, and a total waste of my time.

What was done was done.

At that time, I was naive, new to this hook-up experience, and did not understand that faking who you were and putting your best pics was the thing to do. Some even had the nerve to put pics ten years ago, and girls were okay with it. Not that they had a choice because every chat, every meet was left to chance.

I was still reeling when he led me into the elevator. He was not cool. So not cool. And my mind wasn't letting go.

"Which floor?" He pointed to the buttons.

My hand shook slightly as I scanned my card to the keypad and pushed the number.

He hugged me tight. "I'm so happy I'm here."

He placed his hands on my shoulders and pulled back to stare into my face. "You're so beautiful. More beautiful in person than in our vid chats."

"Oh...thanks." I swallowed. "Thanks for coming over to see me." My throat squeezed. A step at a time, dragging my feet on the carpet. L was oblivious to the storm in my heart.

We walked down the hall as I felt like a prisoner heading to the executioner's block. Yes, it was maybe too much to describe. He wasn't bad looking, but perhaps because I had a deep expectation, and I blamed myself for it. He wasn't my type.

"Remember to do a proper vid chat with the guys," H said a month or two before our Korean trip.

"Do I need to?" I asked.

"Yes. You have to."

"But how do I ask them?"

"You need to protect yourself," he said.

H was right, and I thought I did. L and I had over ten times of vid sex. Why didn't I see him properly?

Because he wore shades, or was quick with flipping his phone to his erection. His face wasn't as important as what we were doing. Or maybe he was worried that I might be a scammer.

Why was I so trusting?

"You are too horny," said H. "Always impatient and desperate to play.

H was right. I was too stubborn to heed his words.

We stepped inside, and L hugged me from behind. I felt his thick erection against my ass, thick and long, and his biceps wound tightly around me.

I was trapped. "I have my period."

Proving again how much I wanted this meeting to work and how much of a sex addict I was becoming, I was willing to do anything to get this guy.

"It's your dream come true," smirked H as I excitedly stepped off the plane ten days before.

"That's okay," L said, and he lifted my green dress and pulled it over my head. I wore a black lingerie under it. Lace one-piece with a T-panty clinging like a lifeline between my crack, highlighting my assets for him to admire.

"Don't you want to eat?" I asked, pointing to the table and the to-go grilled pork dinner I bought for him because he didn't have time to eat.

"Later," he said.

His lips collided with mine. His braces didn't bother me. His hands cupped my ass as he roughly pulled me against him. At six feet plus, 186 cm, he was more than a head taller than me, and I had to tilt my head up to meet him.

"Wait," I said and rushed to the bathroom to grab some towels. Suddenly forgetting that I didn't like him or the surprise he gave me. He was a great kisser, and his hard body against mine aroused my need to fuck.

Fuck it.

So what his face wasn't what I'd expected. I could take him as a one-night stand.

He took his shirt off when I got back. Super nice pecs, smooth and hard all over, tanned but not overly. He had a beautiful body.

L was naughty. Knowing tricks to please and was ready to pound hard into me. We did it two times, and he came twice before we stopped. If I didn't have my period, he'd go down on me. He told me again and again.

We stopped so he could eat. It was tteokbokki sex, and we had to wipe and shower and fucked again, and repeat. Doggy, mission, cowgirl, whatever he wanted, we did. He liked blowjobs, but it would have been the best outdoor as we promised. It was midnight when we stopped. The kinky didn't happen, just good old-fashioned acts of love.

The night was a repeat of my moans, shouts, and his groans. We didn't care who heard or how much we had to clean up. At some point, we stopped, and we both washed up and slept.

There wasn't much talk. Language was a barrier that sex broke. It was my first time sleeping with a stranger overnight. Afraid to snore, afraid to not be the girl he wanted. It was stressful while he slept like an innocent babe.

This was a first for everything. This trip to Dreamland, where all the Korean crazed girls and women wished they had been. And I bagged five. Had them as they had me — the Asian cougar Milf foreigner. Those Korean men that everyone fetishized. It was fun, thrilling, and extremely naughty because the cougar hunted where society frowned.

The verdict was. They weren't different from other men. Good sex was good sex, and some could be better, and some was kind of mind-blowing. As a naive baby cougar, I jumped before I swam.

Team Butt gal. Impulsive as always. Mistakes were learned in the process. The thrill of the unexpected. Heart pounding, body jerking, voices moaning, sweat as slick as raindrops on glass, and hands raised in exhilaration.

Carpe diem. We writers die to live in our words. One day, I wish you'd read this and remember me. My confessions, my love for life, and the young guys who would remember the one time when an Asian Milf blew their world.

LIKE AN ANIMAL

Here we go again.

I want to be more than friends.

Was that what he was implying? Saying that we were fated in our prior lives? Or was he a sweet talker and love bomber?

Having been bitten more than I could be shy, you'd think I'd think twice and more with two years under my belt.

"You are too good. You are too nice," many guys have said before, and minutes or seconds later, these double twisters break me into tiny pieces.

"We'll start with you hurting me first," this new guy said.

Refreshing. Made me feel bad, but maybe this was to put me at ease.

"How can I hurt you when you don't know me?" I said.

"You are meant for me." Dark eyes stare down. "I'm very picky."

Words that could work on any girl. Heart a-fluttering. He was good. Sleek. And probably laughing while reading this.

"I'm sorry, but I can't trust anyone anymore," I replied.

This guy was too sexy right from the get-go. A week before my flight, I saw him on Hinge and got the tingles just listening to his recorded voice.

I wasn't gonna fall for this again. My quest to find that perfect pervert got close once, till I was burned.

I didn't blame the first guy. I broke him as he broke me. Stories to come and lessons not learned.

Again and again, in that merry-go-round hunt and prance, I was no better than I was when I first started. Looking back, as the loop connected, I was better off at first than now. At least then, I had a clear goal and knew what I wanted.

Perverts unite, perverts rule.

I wasn't a teacher. I was no one's mommy. I had needs and sought like-minded horny guys to fulfill them.

Was there such a thing as a sexual mind match? Mind, body, and lust? Was it possible for people to find more than one best match and mate? Or is this attraction going to fizzle out as fast as you fucked?

The match is lit. How long could this new fire burn?

"I wish I had met you a month before you left," he said.

"Yes. Me too."

In that month, we could have satiated everything buried in us. Multiple orgasms and mind-blowing sex later, we could be normal people. Finally, we are getting all that angst out of our heads and from every nook and cranny of ourselves. Experiment as we want and do all the things we could only dream of for the longest time.

He'd be my best partner. Refreshing and willing. The master that this pet needed. The animal that bit my breasts and inner thighs, leaving marks and bruises for a week.

"They're huge!" I told him. "Anyone who sees these will know what you did."

"Let them see." He smirked.

Yeah, he knew what he wanted. He marked me, and any guys who came after would be seconds.

"You're a cannibal. You're eating me alive!" I sighed.

His smirk was beyond sexy. It drove me insane. These two

months in Asia will be the longest test for something that has barely started.

"For once, I didn't want to go," I told him, teary-eyed, the day before. Even H wouldn't believe this if I told him.

Korea was my Mecca, and I'd crave it until I was bored and sad. It was the one place that I set my mind on after summer ended. A goal to aim for the rest of the year till next summer came. Maybe when I return home this year, I won't pine for Korea anymore.

"You're always obsessive," H said. "Always too passionate, sprinting without thinking until you fall."

Inside and out. And my next fixation may be dirty, hot Chinese guys.

And so this is my confession to you — my sexy, racy perv — the animal who left his virus in me. Poison is turning my blood into yours. Two monsters in a world of sanity. You match all my needs, and I, Milfy Cougar, am being bitten and caught by you, an unexpected, seemingly casual, friendly guy.

We are more than what others perceive. There is a dark attraction and animal instinct in all of us. The question is how much of that raw hunger exists and how beaten down we are by our society, culture, and lives to be free.

I want some more. So, I'll let you take a bite of my ass tonight.

I eat young men for breakfast, lunch, and maybe dinner.

It used to be fun. Watching these guys turn from innocence into ragged, mindlessly horny wolves, wanting to strip my clothes off and using me to feed their hunger.

But last year mellowed. The young ones drowned by life weren't as passionate as I hoped, and with each conquest, my flames slowly dissipated.

Animal guy's arms had the habit of wrapping my shoulders and squeezing me against his chest. It was our first meeting, and we were strolling like lovers in a park. His eyes never left my face. Every second I breathed and glanced over, his eyes were there, on me.

"Why are you staring at me?" I asked.

"Why aren't you using your cougar's playbook on me?" He asked.

"Because I don't want to," I replied.

"Why?"

"Do you want to be like the others?" I asked.

"No. But I'm curious."

"Please me, and I'll show you some," I giggled. I didn't tell him that I thought he was too special for that and that it wasn't necessary to test him because I already knew he'd fit. Our wavelengths were in sync when we met and chatted about my stories and other stuff.

He was a dirty pervert, with our similar-minded fetishes for outdoor kinks and flashing BDSM fun, I knew. Under his cheekiness, he was what I wanted. Everything else about him was icing on the cake.

So, what are you waiting for?

And, finally, he asked. "Want to go to my place? My brother and sister-in-law are away."

In his car and on our way, I said I was hot, took off my bra, and tossed it on his lap. His hand stretched and was stuck to my lap, stroking my smooth, pale leg up and down like waves on shore.

My panties were wet from sweat and his endless touch. We got to his place and beelined to his couch. Or did I fall into it, or did he push me into it?

The details didn't matter. His lips were on mine. Experienced, soft, and firm. Tongue twisting and our breath as one. He flipped me over, pillows tossed aside.

Black dress pulled down to the waist and skirt lifted up. My huge ass faced him as he hooked his fingers on my black, laced T-panties and pulled me down to my knees.

His first slap came as a clap of thunder. Echoing up the high ceilings of the living room and the stairs.

I gasped loudly, and then it came again — the feel of his hard palm on my meaty flesh. The jiggle of my ass didn't stop the pain from spreading from the points of contact. The lightning edges of his fingertips spread in concentric circles.

"Are you okay?" he asked.

"More…" I whispered. "More…"

He didn't stop. Each smack was followed by my moans, and as they got harder and louder, my voice became screams. With one hand on my hip, the other invading my wet pussy, each stroke was struck with maximum pain and pleasure. Fingers thrusting, timing attacks to my senses, driving me insane with waves of feelings.

"So sexy…" he groaned. His pants dropped, and his underwear pulled down. He was rubbing his hard cock against my skin and teasing my tender, moist parts.

His lips were on my neck, running down my back. He was pulling my hair like a leash, jerking my hair back as he entered and hammered into me hard. Riding me, flesh slapping against flesh. Wet and slippery with each stroke, hands alternating between squeezing my ass and spanking. My head was reeling.

"I feel so dizzy…" I moaned.

"You like it?" His lips against my ear. His voice could make me cum. Smooth and deep, stroking my thoughts, mentally rubbing my clit to ecstasy.

"Yes…please…more…spank me…" I begged.

He flipped me and pushed me up the sofa. His head dropped down.

I felt shy as he kissed my body, running down till he reached his goal. Tongue licking and lips smacking my inner thighs, and then, teeth.

My mind was reeling. I couldn't think. Mindless.

I won't get out of this alive. I want some more.

You're killing me now.

The animals inside of me and you.

Here we go again.

Let us burn our hearts tonight.

—o THOUGHTS o—

A new year is about to start, and here I'm writing the ending to this book. Three years is a long time to confess to. From the beginning of Yolo-ing, I knew I had to write this. An otherworldly call to my soul telling me I had to leave my mark.

Perhaps it was a cry for help from the people who confided in me. Their stories, our conversations, and our acts of lust blended into real fiction that you get to read today. The stories appear on my site first because making a book is an tenacious process, while blog-style reads are free for those seeking some entertainment.

"Your stories are more polished and well-written than I thought," said many guys. They could have been trying to get me into their sheets. But the fact was, I was fishing them and bringing them to my site, as I searched for ways to bring my female readers to the same point.

Sex shouldn't be shamed. Cums and orgasms should be celebrated. Nature brings us together to procreate. To enjoy the fruits of our pounding labor with highs that no drugs or anything else can achieve.

And if you think this is really the end — no. Most things come in pairs. Hands, feet, and two bodies melting into one.

Mom by day, Cougar by night — not all things are rosy. Thorns bleed, and so do tears.

To more days and nights of dirty, sexy fun, and sad goodbyes. When the moon sleeps, the sun will rise.

—oo—

HAPPY ENDINGS NEVER END

—oo—

—oo—

To all the guys I'd chatted with, met,
And the lucky few whom I played with.
I won't forget you.
You who were written from my thoughts,
Thank you.
xoxoxo
Byeon Byeon

—oo—